Birth
of a
Goddess

Tristan R. Waters

For my daughters Namine, Haylee, and Jessie, who are always with me even when we are not together.

Introduction

Greetings. The tale of Syry and her legacy was written to give history, depth, and origin to a character that will influence my later writings. However, at times you may find a lack of information; this was done on purpose for two main reasons: firstly, the development of Syry'scharacter is central to my writing, and secondly, I needed a way of presenting my thoughts and my ideas of who and what this character is. Something else that her story has allowed me to do is to give further depth and background to my writing, along with a general working history of the world I created for Syry's story and the stories to come.

I have included two appendices: Appendix A covers general knowledge, terminology, and further details about the world in which this story occurs; Appendix B describes some of the characters. However, a word of warning: both appendices contain spoilers, so use them cautiously. In Appendix B, you will find missing information about some characters; I did this on purpose to add a little more openness with the characters but also to allow readers to visualize what characters look like and to make the tale a creation of their imagination.

Lastly, a note about the map: the place names include lakes, rivers, coastal bays, mountains and landforms, castles, towns, cities, and other points of interest. A few map locations are at the same point, so you may see them as 1/1, indicating they are of the same name type, or a-1 or

1A-1, indicating they are of two name types, such as 6A: Ben Macdui and 1: Lelen Alora.

So, please enjoy the tale of Syry.

Map Index

Lakes, Rivers, and Coastal Bays

a.   Scapa Bay; A7/8
b.   Whalsay Bay; B1/2
c.   Stormwater Bay; A6
d.   Thurso River; A6-C4
e.   Handa Bay; B4
f.   Cawdor Bay; B5/6
g.   Loch Dornoch; C5
h.   Loch Moray; C5
i.   Loch Ness; C4/5
j.   Tummel River; C5-E5/6
k.   Loch Hourn; D4
l.   Awe River; D5-E4/5
m.   Loch Tay; D6
n.   Bay of Firth of Forth; E6
o.   Aman River; E5-G6
p.   Ka'leen Bay; E4/5
q.   Lough Magheramore; F3
r.   Drumard Bay; G2
s.   Lough Strangford; G4
t.   Brodik Bay; F5/6
u.   Cromer Bay; F7/8
v.   Norwich Bay; G9
w.   Shannon River; F3-I3
x.   Lough Claire; G2-H2
y.   Wicklow Bay; G4
z.   Bangor Bay; G6
aa.   Trent River; G7-H7
bb.   Lough Ardbear; H2
cc.   Corrib River; H3
dd.   Lough Liscasey; I1
ee.   Firth of Clyde; H4
ff.   Mersey Bay; H5/6
gg.   Yarmouth Bay; H9
hh.   Telford Lake; H6-I6
ii.   Thames River; I7-K8/9
jj.   Bath River; I6-J5
kk.   Cardigan Bay; J3/4
ll.   Bristol Bay; J5-K5
mm.   Ramsgate Bay; J9

Mountains and Landforms

1A.   Orkney Isles; A7/8
2A.   Shetland Isles; B1/2
3A.   Ben Rimsdale; A5
4A.   Ben More Assynt; B5
5A.   Ben Wyvis; B5
6A.   Ben Macdui; C6
7A.   Ounich Mountain; D4
8A.   Humber Mountain; F7
9A.   Valhalla; G3
10A.   Isle of Manx; G5
11A.   The Twins; G1/2
12A.   Forge Mountain; G8
13A.   Silver Fire Mount; G8
14A.   Mount Naas; H3
15A.   Ben Tynt Tees; H6
16A.   Mount Ennis; I2
17A.   Trowbridge Mountain; I5
18A.   Walford Mountain; J7
19A.   Bristol Mountain; K5
20A.   Càrn Eige; D4

Castle, Towns, and Cities

1. Lelen Alora; C6
2. Perth; D6
3. Yalnora; D4
4. Leven; E6
5. Alloa; E5
6. Sitthi; E6
7. Sitthi Castle; E6
8. Ket; E4
9. Totia; E5
10. Lo'karan; F5
11. Derry; F4
12. Dunnagall; G2
13. Ardara; G2
14. Ta'neek; H6
15. Kent; G7

Points of Interest

A1. Syry's Landing; F5
B1. Battle against General Danner

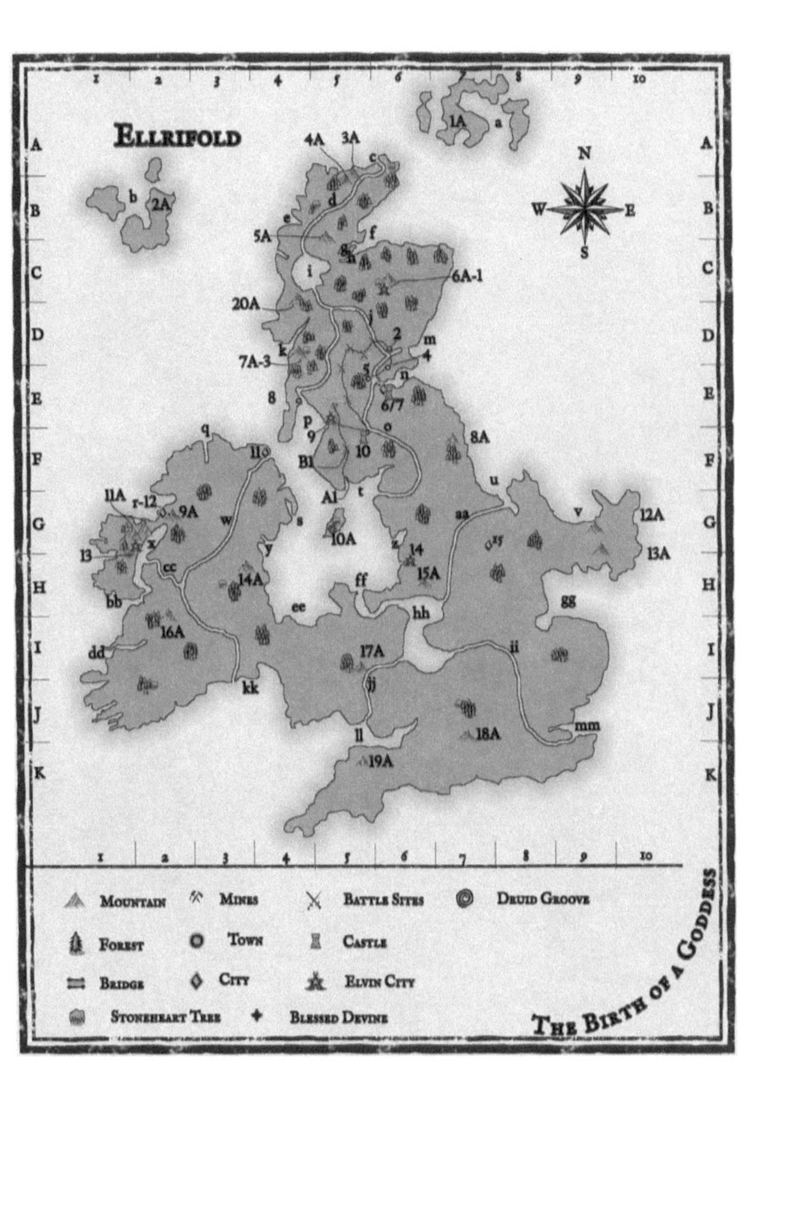

Ellrifold
THE BIRTH OF A GODDESS
N
W
E
S
Mountain
Forest
Bridge
Stoneheart Tree
Mines
Town
City
Battle Sites
Castle
Elvin City
Blessed Devine
Druid Groove

Chapter 1

A Heron and a Child

For nearly a thousand years, I have lived and walked the lands of Ellrifold, but now that my age and my past are catching up with me, I feel that I must tell the story of someone whom I held dear, someone whom I loved as if she were my blood, someone whom I would have killed for and someone whom I would have died for. The first time I laid eyes on her and held her, she was already a few months old.

Our story begins with the Sitthi Kingdom that ruled about 250 miles north and south of the ocean bay of Firth of Forth and to the western shores of Ellrifold, including the Elven kingdom of Totia. Most elven people followed their clan elders, but a king and queen ruled the Totia Kingdom, and they were well-loved and respected.

Unfortunately, in 1215, just the year before Syry was born in 1216, Koyla, the king of the Sitthi Kingdom, had crushed the forces of Totia. Having captured the king and queen, Koyla executed the king in front of the remainder of his people to ensure that the elven folk knew they had been defeated. Koyla's iron fist was evident at the king's execution when he forced the queen, who was several months with child, to lap at the pooling blood of her husband as he stood over her with his sword lying across her back. The spectacle drew much anger from the defeated people who were forced to witness the execution.

Here is how I met Syry and the beginning of her tale.

It was just a few days after the first spring thaws of 1216 of the elven calendar, and I was traveling at the southern tip of the Sitthi Kingdom. It was nearly dark when I heard the slight rustling of a bush and a baby's faint cry. At first, I gave it no mind, but the crying did not subside.

As I parted the bushes and peered among them, I found an elven woman. She had a deep wound in her left side just below the last rib and was clutching a baby. It frightened her when she saw me, but she soon realized I was not a threat.

"Child, come let me help you," I told her. It is funny thinking back now at the word 'child.' My people often used the word child for elven, dwarf, orc, and human races because they were often much younger than my people, the Uthuk-Nari.

"Uthuk, take my child and flee; leave me behind," she whispered.

As I crouched beside her, I saw a tattoo of heron on her neck just below her jaw and realized who she was. "You are Ella, the fallen queen."

She nodded. Breathing shallowly, she replied, "Yes. Please take my daughter and flee from here."

"Ella, I can take her and deliver her to your people to the south."

"Wait," she said. "I have met you before, have not I?"

"Yes, some eighty years ago."

"A'con… No, that is not right, A'kull, correct?"

"Yes, A'kull is my name."

"Please, A'kull, take Syry and protect her. I can only trust one of the uthuk-nari to protect her from Koyla."

I knew that by taking Syry, I would be forced to keep a secret that was not mine to tell. Even so, I said, "Very well, Ella. I will take her and protect her as if she were my own. While I cannot bury you or burn your remains to spread at a Stoneheart Tree, at least let me give you peace."

She nodded, then placed a soft kiss upon Syry's head before I slipped a small, thin blade between her ribs directly into her heart. As I pulled the blade free, she drew her last breath; she was now at peace.

I stowed my blade as I closed her eyes. After I crossed Ella's arms over her chest, I gathered the now-sleeping Syry and fixed a sling to hold her close to me. I did my best to conceal Ella's body so she would not be disturbed. After doing so, I turned south because it was the shortest distance out of the Sitthi Kingdom and quickly jogged away while Syry slept on. Due to my people's abilities, I did not stop moving until the sun rose from the east, and Syry stirred in her sling for the first time.

I did not know then how much love and devotion I would have for my young charge. At first, I only saw Syry as a charge that needed my protection and nothing more, but that would change.

I stayed off the main roads for almost a fortnight because I was unsure if Kolya had hunters looking for Ella and Syry. I knew I needed to feed Syry, so I often found small homesteads well away from towns or cities with cows or sheep. Thankfully, most of the farms I went to were more than willing to offer milk, and thankfully, they did not ask any questions.

Chapter 2

A Tailor or a Mage

A month had passed since that fateful evening that I had met Syry. She changed as we traveled further south, becoming more used to being on the move with me. I knew that at some point, we would come across a guard patrol or have to enter a town. One of uthuk-naris' abilities is altering our appearance; some have mastered this and can drastically change our looks. I could take on a new face if I wished, including changing the shape of my ears or even the color of my eyes. Most of the time, I kept my ears rounded like a human's because it drew the least attention, especially with my hair cut short. I was grateful that Syry's hair was long enough to cover the tips of her elvish ears.

The time to keep our distance from cities or towns ended when we came to the walled city of Kent. Even though we had not been followed, I needed to know if any word had spread south about the missing queen and her young daughter.

Long before we entered the city, I made my face and eyes look more human instead of their normal cat-like appearance. I also shortened my height, an ability that I alone have mastered; typically, my people are anywhere between seven and nearly ten feet tall, and I stand at almost eight feet.

Even though Kent was a small city, it did a lot of trade inside and outside its stone walls. As we mixed with the travelers waiting to be admitted into the city, I ensured that my cloak covered Syry, who was asleep. I was also thankful that my only weapons were the fighting blade I carried across my back and my dirk, which was sheathed on my left hip just underneath the baby but still accessible if the need arose.

As we moved slowly towards the gate, I heard that there was a toll to enter the city, which did not surprise me. I also listened for any word from the north.

"What brings you here, traveler?" asked a guard near the gate.

"Need a wash, a change of clothing, and a bed," I replied.

The guard looked me up and down before he responded, "What is under the cloak?" As he asked me, his left hand touched the hilt of his sword.

"My daughter," I replied, partially opening my cloak to reveal a sleeping Syry.

"Styqgeni," the guard commanded.

As I fumbled in my coin pouch, I remarked how Kent had changed. "The charge has gone up since I last passed through here."

"Well, if you are not careful, it will be a stosakel," he retorted.

I pulled the coin out and laid three shillings in his palm. Two shillings equals a styqgeni, but the third was to keep him from prying into why a lone man was traveling with a baby and to keep him quiet.

Once we passed the gates, we headed for the Silken Seam, a small tailor shop off the main square. This quaint little place was run by an elderly elven couple who took great pride in their work. As I pushed open the door, a small brass bell rang, signaling to the owners that a patron was waiting.

"Welcome, please come in. What can I help you with today?" asked an elven man as he was packing customers' orders.

"I am in search of clothing that would fit a baby."

"Is there anything else?"

"Can you recommend someone who can make a carrying sling for a baby?" I asked as I pulled the edge of my cloak back to reveal Syry's makeshift sling.

"Tina, come here, please!" shouted the man, tilting his head towards a curtain leading into another room.

A woman came through. "Yes, Hal? Oh, hello," she said to me. "What do you need?"

Even though the question was addressed to her husband, I replied. "I need a sling made for a baby."

For the first time since entering the room, Tina took notice of Syry lying in the sling I had fashioned. She moved closer to get a better look."That it is a simple job. Hal, can you go to the market and see if that dwarf has arrived?" She turned to me. "Now, please follow me."

Hal nodded and headed for the front door. As Hal left, Tina went back through the curtain. I followed into another room. The walls were covered with bolts of cloth and wooden cubbies. "Do you have any particular cloth in mind for the sling?" she asked.

"Just something strong but lightweight."

"Elven silk would be the best for that, but it is not cheap."

"Coin is not a problem, Tina."

"Very well. Is there a particular color you want?" She waved her hand at the wall to my right, and I looked briefly at the colors before selecting a dark blue that would blend with my clothing.

"This one," I pointed.

"Would you mind taking the baby out and laying them on the table so I can measure them?"

At first, I did not want to, for secrecy about Syry's identity was paramount, but in the end, I lifted her out. She woke up and babbled a bit as I laid her down.

Tina pulled the cloth bolt off the wall and came over to take the measurements. "You have a beautiful daughter…" she remarked, looking into Syry's royal-blue eyes. Then she stroked Syry's cheek, making the baby giggle slightly, which caused her elven ears to poke out for her fire-kissed blond hair.

"Wait! She is not your daughter; she is an elf! Where did you take her from?" Before Tina turned to look at me, I allowed myself to return to my natural state. She was shocked to see how much taller I suddenly was.

"Before you say another word, let me explain," I begged.

"Come towards me, and I will scream."

I stayed where I was and asked. "Do you know who or what I am?"

"Some sort of wizard," she retorted.

"My people are the uthuk-nari, and this child is someone I was entrusted to protect."

"What of her parents?"

"Dead, both of them…"

Tina gestured towards Syry. "Does she have a name?"

"She does, but I will not disclose it until we are further away from where she has been."

Tina did not reply for a moment as she pondered. Finally, she said, "If you fear something, you must come from the north out of Sitthi?"

"Yes."

"I would not ask anything further of you."

"Thank you, Tina."

"I am guessing you also need clothes for her besides the sling?"

"Yes."

"I will make you a few sets for her, including changing clothes."

"Thank you. How much for everything?" I asked.

"Two pounds. I can have everything ready by morning."

"That will be good."

I was pulling the coin out of my pouch when Tina stopped me. "Pay me when you collect your items. Now, please let me measure her."

I pulled a step back or two, allowing her to move closer. Just as she finished, her husband came in looking almost ragged. "Hal, what is it?" she demanded.

"In the market, I overheard someone talking about how Queen Ella and her daughter have managed to escape."

At that, I turned towards the door and muttered, "Damn! I never should have come here." Hal looked at Syry lying on the table where Tina was measuring her.

"Hal," the woman asked, "did you recognize the speaker?"

"No, I did not, but judging by his clothes, I would say he comes from the north."

I interrupted them. "Tina, have you gotten your measurements? I need to get her out of sight."

"Yes, I have. Hal, open the door to below."

"Below?" I asked as Hal pulled aside one of the fabric cases to reveal a flight of stairs leading downwards. "What is going on here?" I asked.

"I once served Queen Ella and her husband, King Danu," Tina responded. "Even though I left their service, I still have a sense of duty toward them. And, if I am correct judging by the change in your mood, this is Ella and Danu's daughter."

"Yes, she is, Tina, and now you understand why I need to get her out of sight."

Tina picked up Syry and handed her to me. "Take her below. Both of you will be safe there - no one knows about this passage. Once we close this evening, I will fetch you."

"Thank you, Tina, and you, Hal." They both nodded curtly, and I descended the narrow steps carved into the ground.

There was a faint yellow-white glow above me from simple quartz crystals or mage lites that illuminated our descent. It did not take long to reach the bottom, where I found a large room almost the same size as the building above; like the passageway, its ceiling was lined with the same crystals.

While it was cool down below, it was not freezing. After a while, I removed my cloak, laid it on the floor, and placed Syry on it. I removed my weapons and put them within easy reach before laying down next to Syry and staring at the flickering crystal ceiling.

I must have fallen asleep. I did not know how much time had passed before Tina came down to us, but it was nightfall when we ascended the stairs.

Tina gently nudged my leg. "Wake up, friend. It is safe for the time being."

"Did anyone come looking for us?"

"No one paid us a visit." She offered me her hand to help me up. I did not need her help, but I accepted her hand for a different reason. Not all of my people can read other people's minds with a simple touch, but I have that ability, although I rarely use it. As my hand met her forearm, she returned my grip, and I started seeing flashes of memories. Most people never knew I could see into their minds, but Tina was not like most people.

"Bloody ancestors!" she shrieked as she felt my presence in her mind.

"Was your name Neela when you served Ella?"

"How…? What did you do to me?"

"I was trying to read your memories."

"You could have asked!" she protested.

"I could have, but I doubt you would have told me the truth. I am sorry, Tina. Most people are not aware of my presence."

"Maybe, maybe not. Neela was a long time ago and had a different life. What made you try and read my mind?"

"The crystals," I pointed up at them. "I have met many people who can make ones as good as these, but the cost is high, and I doubt that you and Hal could have afforded them - unless you made them yourselves."

"Yes, I did craft them, though now I rarely use that art."

I picked up Syry, who was wide awake. "She seems to be hungry," Tina said. "Come. Hal is tending to dinner, and we have some fresh milk for her."

I gathered my cloak and weapons as she approached the stairs and followed her. "Tina, why did you create the space below your shop?"

"Hal and I made it for the exact reason I showed it to you."

"To hide?"

"Correct. Over the years, we have made every effort possible to help those fleeing the enslaved northern kingdoms. Thankfully, no one has ever discovered what we do."

We were back on the shop's main floor and walked into the small kitchen, where they ate. As we entered the doorway, I had to duck a little to keep from hitting my head on the door frame. Hal was pouring the stew he had made into three small bowls. As I sat on one of the stools, Tina was filling a leather bottle with milk for Syry, who eagerly reached for it.

"Silly girl, always hungry," I remarked.

"What is her name?" Tina asked.

For a long moment, I debated whether to tell them her name or give them a lie. "Syry," I said.

"Beautiful name…"

"Tina, Hal, forgive me. I am A'kull."

"A'kull? That sounds familiar, but I cannot place it," Hal stated as he pondered my name.

"The Butcher of Ka'leen Bay, Hal," Tina remarked.

"You are not old enough to have been there, Tina," I remarked.

"No, I was not old enough, but my mother was in the village at the time and told me many times about the events of that day."

"Refresh my memory about what happened," Hal asked, and Tina looked at me.

"It happened a long time ago, Hal, over a hundred years…" While the event and its consequences never bothered me, it still was not something I wanted to dredge up. "I had been hunting a man named Hess and his band of fifty or sixty warriors for some time. Finally, one spring, I tracked them to the village of Ket in Ka'leen Bay, where Hess was more or less keeping the villagers prisoner. I shadowed the village, learning about the villagers and seeing if any prisoners could help me. There was one, an orc, who gladly joined my side."

"Before the bloodbath started, I walked out of the mist that covered the village and the bay to the center where Hess was eating. At first, he laughed at me for coming alone. I offered him a chance to surrender, but he ordered his men to attack. None of them truly wanted to fight me, but in the end, they came… The orc caught them by surprise, and – though he assisted me, the fight cost him his life. By the time the mist had cleared that morning, every warrior that served Hess was hewn to pieces; Hess himself was missing his right arm below the elbow, and his left leg was cut to the bone. Thankfully, none of the villagers lost their lives."

"Did all of Hess's band deserve to die?" Hal asked.

"Yes. They had been killing, raping, pillaging, and more for years. Several lands had a price on his head, but nobody had ever got close to killing Hess and his men because of their sheer numbers."

"It sounds like they deserved what they got," stated Hal, nodding in agreement.

"Do either of you know a man named Ha'thap?"I asked.

"I believe he owns the blacksmith's shop at the other end of town, although we have never had business with him."

I was thankful that neither Tina nor Hal had asked me about my business with Ha'thap. After my story about Hess, we sat down and ate a simple meal; only after we had finished did I tell them I needed to leave.

Chapter 3

Family

After the meal, I gathered my cloak and Syry, ready to find Ha'thap's shop. However, Tina approached me before I put Syry in my makeshift sling. "A'kull, I finished the sling for you. You can tie it where it will carry her near your waist or to your chest."

"Thank you, Tina."

"Pay me when you collect the last of your order, which I will have finished in the morning."

"Thank you again. I will not return tonight, but I will return in the morning."

Without saying anything further, I placed Syry in the new sling, a significant improvement over the makeshift one I had fashioned.

The black night encompassed everything as I slipped from Tina and Hal's shop. A few torches had been lit, but it was relatively dark, so I could move without fear of being seen.

It did not take me long to reach the other side of Kent, let alone find Ha'thap's blacksmith shop. When I neared the door, I saw the faint glow of the forge peeking out from underneath the door, but I could not hear the sound of iron being hammered.

I knocked lightly upon the door and waited for it to be answered. Soon, the door was cracked open, and I found myself staring at a boy no older than thirteen. "Can I help you, sir?" he squeaked.

"Is Ha'thap home?"

"Yes..." Before he could say anything else, I heard Ha'thap's barrel of a voice shouting from somewhere in the back of the shop.

"Who is at the door, Tee?"

"Someone who is asking for you," young Tee yelled to his mentor.

"Let them in."

Tee opened the door and allowed me to enter. As I walked into the room, Ha'thap came through from the back of the shop.

"Brother, it has been too long." Like myself, Ha'thap stood more than seven feet tall and was solid and stout like the rest of our people. We approached each other and embraced in a bear-like hug.

"Hap, it has indeed been too long," I said. Hap was the name that he went by among friends and family.

"Have you eaten supper?" he asked.

"Yes, I have."

"Well, no matter. Come, Arawa will be glad to see you." Hap turned and went through a door that led to his home at the back and above his shop. As we entered the kitchen, Hap's wife, Arawa, was cutting up a pig roast for dinner.

"A'kull! I would hug and kiss you, but my hands are covered in pig."

"No matter, Arawa, you can do that later." I removed my cloak to reveal Syry sitting in the sling, looking at the world around her.

"Well, what is this?" Hap asked.

"It is a tale for sure. This is Syry, someone whom I was entrusted to protect."

"A tale I am sure will be told in time," retorted Arawa.

"Yes," I replied.

As Hap helped Arawa finish preparing their meal, I sat at their table and balanced Syry on my leg as she grabbed and tried munching on some bread. While they ate their dinner, I told them how Syry came into my care and that I wanted to get as far away from Sitthi as possible. Hap and Arawa were sad to hear of Ella's passing but were glad she had gotten her daughter out of the hell that surrounded the Sitthi realm.

"What are your plans for the time being, A'kull?" asked Arawa after I finished telling them how Syry came into my care.

"I am thinking that the safest place to take her would be to Bliźniacy, the home of our people," I replied.

"Going by land will take you the better part of the year to reach," stated Hap.

"After I leave here in the morning, I was planning on heading to the coast and getting passage on a ship."

"Smart… Do you know if he is looking for them?" Hap asked without naming who, but I knew who he was referring to.

"I am not sure, but if I happened a guess, it would be yes, and all the more reason to get as far away as possible," suddenly, there was a hard knock on the door, which made all of us tense, and me reaching for the blade on my back.

"No, Tee, stay here. I will see who it is?" Hap ordered. As Hal neared the entry door, he picked up a smithy hammer. Then a hard knock came again and a shout.

"Come on, open the damn door, Hap!" I could see that Hap lowered the hammer to his side as he reached for the locking bolt and was no longer tense.

"Tah'kainn, Da'kian, what are you two doing here?" Hap asked as he looked through the door opening.

"Well, will you let us in, or shall we stand here all night?" asked Da'kian.

"Sorry," Hap stepped aside as he opened the door, letting them enter. As they both entered Hap's forge room, they removed their cloaks, revealing both of them wearing the steel plate armor of my people. While the armor was heavy, it still allowed complete movement of the body, and with the aid of the various gambeson and mail, it was almost impenetrable. "How did you get through the gate at this hour?"

"Coin, and a fair bit of it," replied Tah'kainn.

"Then I know who is commanding the gate, the ass he is," retorted Hap as Tah'kainn and Da'kian hung their cloaks on one of the posts near the shop's entry. "Come, you two are not our only guests tonight."

As they entered the kitchen, they found Arawa holding the knife she used to carve the pig and me standing with my blade drawn. We both put our blades down once we saw who had come in.

"A'kull, where have you been the past few years?" asked Tah'kainn.

"I have been busy. What brings you here at this hour?" I replied.

"We hoped you might have heard the news of the fallen Queen Ella and her daughter. They escaped Koyla's grasp...." As Da'kian was still speaking, I lifted Syry from the chair I had placed her on.

"Well, I can help answer your question. But, first, Tah'kainn and Da'kian, allow me to introduce Syry, the daughter of Queen Ella and King Danu."

"Where is her mother?" asked Da'kian.

"Dead, I am afraid. I found Ella deeply wounded and holding Syry. Ella asked me on her dying breath to protect Syry, and I will do so. What have you two heard about her escape?" As I asked Tah'kainn and Da'kian, they sat at the table, and Arawa placed two clean plates and cups and gestured for them to join them at dinner.

"To the north and almost everywhere we have been the past ten days, we keep hearing of or seeing people hunting for them, as Koyla has staked a $10,000 gold pound price on their heads," replied Tah'kainn.

"Getting as far away as possible seems even more so than before. So we will leave and head for the coast and a ship in the morning," I retorted.

"A'kull, we will come with you if that is no problem?" asked Da'kian.

"I will always welcome my brothers to join me in travel," I replied.

"Do you have a horse, A'kull?" asked Tah'kainn.

"No, I have been on foot for some time."

"There is a horse farm just outside the city; you can get a horse there," stated Hap as he tore into a chunk of bread.

"Very good. I have one stop in the morning, and then we can leave."

"What stop is that A'kull?" asked Tah'kainn.

"The tailors, I ordered clothes for Syry. She has been wearing the same clothes since I found them. I think I will turn in; I have been up for several days with little rest."

"I will show you where you can rest for the night," said Arawa as we both got up.

"Hap, do you still have the bows?" I asked Hap as I stepped away from the table.

"I do; I will get one out for you by morning."

"Thank you." I followed Arawa up a small flight of stairs to a large open second floor with only curtains dividing the area. "Arawa, thank you. This will do for the night."

"You are welcome. A'kull, is everything all right? You seem troubled?"

"It has been so long since I have had to care for someone, and I do not feel that I am ready or worthy of to."

"I am sorry, A'kull. I have forgotten about your loss," replied Arawa.

"It is all right, Arawa…."

"A'kull, you were a wonderful father and husband and will be again."

"Maybe."

"I will leave you two be," Arawa hugged and kissed me on the cheek, leaving us to settle for the night.

Chapter 4

A Promise Broken

The night quickly slipped by for us as we slept in the home of my brother Ha'thap and his wife, Arawa. However, as the sun was breaking the eastern horizon, a half dozen riders rode hard up to the gates of Kent and demanded entrance into the city, while the city guard would normally never allow mounts inside the walls. This time, they made an exception. Once the gates opened wide enough for the riders to pass through, they headed directly for the blacksmith shop of Ha'thap. As they rode up to the shop, the lead rider did not even wait for his horse to come to a complete stop for him to dismount. After dismounting, he headed straight for the door and began hammering on it, trying to gain the attention of Ha'thap or Arawa; an answer came shortly.

"Bloody ancestors! Who is at my door banging away?" Ha'thap moaned as he hurriedly walked to his door, but the hammering did not let up. "I am a coming, dammit! Who the hell is hammering at my door?" Hap roared as he slammed the door bolt back and swung the door open. "Unka! What the hell." Hap did not even see the other riders as they were dismounting.

"Hap, where is he?"

"Where is who, Unka?"

"You know damn well who!" retorted Unka as he tried stepping through the door, but Hap stood firm.

"Again, Unka, who are you looking for?" demanded Hap.

"A'kull. I know he is here," stated Unka.

"He is upstairs asleep," replied Hap.

"Go wake him," without acknowledging Unka, Hap turned around and came to wake me.

A short time later, Hap and I arrived downstairs and entered the forge room, where Unka, Vah'tial, T'hetha, Sewa, Ochui, and Ankou waited for us to return. Before anyone could react, Unka grabbed me and slammed me into a nearby post hard enough to knock the dust loose.

"Where is she?" asked Unka as he shouted at me.

"Where is who?" I asked back while trying to loosen his grip on my tunic.

"You damn well know who?" Unka then pulled me towards him and lightly slammed me against the post.

"Again, who are you asking of me?" I asked again, but Ankou spoke up before Unka could ask again or slam me against the post.

"A'kull, where is the princess?"

"Princess?" this time, Unka threw me across the room, sending me into the anvil, almost knocking it over. Before Unka could get his hands on me again, Ochui, the oldest of the group, stepped in front of him and barred him from laying his hands on me again. "I do not know who you are talking about?"

"Queen Ella's daughter, we know you have her," stated Ochui.

"How do you know that?" Ochui turned to me before responding.

"We found her body, and we found this." Ochui presented my silver raven skull that generally hung from a chain around my neck.

"How?" I immediately touched my neck, not realizing that the chain and skull were missing. "Yes, she is here, but I will not hand her over to you," while I talked, Ochui handed me my raven skull.

"Do not worry, A'kull. We are not here to take her back or away from you," stated Unka.

"Then why are all of you here, Unka?" I asked.

"Kolya has put a $100,000 gold pound price on her and the child's heads. There are dozens of bounty hunters scouring the land for them," stated Ochui.

"Do you know if he knows where they are?" I asked.

"We do not know. However, we have taken care of burning Queen Ella's remains with the druids' help. They have taken care of burying her ashes at a Stoneheart Tree."

"Thank you. I did not do it for fear of Kolya's people possibly being too close," I replied.

"A'kull, we need to leave for her safety. The sooner, the better," stated Unka.

"Well, I was planning on leaving today anyway, but I need to take care of a stop before we can. There is also the matter of me not having a horse."

"Unka, Vah'tial, Ankou, see to a mount for him. The rest of us will go with A'kull and the Princess." With a simple nod from Unka, Vah'tial, and Ankou, they obeyed Ochui's orders and left Hap's shop.

"Wait here. I will go and get her," I stated as I turned away from Ochui. Hap did as well, following a step behind.

"Brother, come with me before you get her," commanded Hap. I almost questioned Hap but did not.

Once we were through the doorway to the kitchen, Hap pulled a case of shelves hinged on the wall just a few feet from the door. Once opened, it revealed a set of stairs leading down. Hap picked up a small oil lamp and led the way down. The stairs opened up to a room almost directly under the forge room supported by thick, heavy oak posts and beam construction. Hap had stopped halfway across the room and lit a sizeable single oil lamp that illuminated the area quite nicely. It took a moment for my eyes to adjust, but once they did, I was staring at the back wall lined with several suits of armor and various weapons among them.

"You have kept them all these years?" I asked.

"Yes. I was not about to destroy some of my best work." Hap replied.

It had been nearly sixty years since I had last donned or seen my armor and swords that Hap had made for me. After walking to the armor stands, I stopped at the second from left and slowly ran my hands over the Valhalla-forged plate armor. Valhalla-forged weapons and armor are made of half trinthi'ium and half steel. Trinthi'ium is lighter and far stronger than steel, but when mixed with steel, it allows the smith to work more manageably.

"I repaired the gambeson and the damaged mail links, but otherwise, it is how you left it."

"Thank you, brother. I swore I would never don this armor again. Now it seems I am about to break that promise," I lowered my head, resting my chin on my chest, slowly shaking my head as I did not want to break my vow. It seemed I had little choice now.

"I do not think Ma'yta would mind considering what is at stake," stated Hap. Ma'yta was my wife, whom I had lost many years ago.

"Maybe? I went to war for her and our girls. I made her that promise as she lay dying in my arms," I still could not bring myself to touch my old armor.

"A'kull, you got your revenge and the justice they deserved, and when the war finished, you kept your word about laying down your arms and armor and moving on, but now someone needs your protection," retorted Hap.

"True, brother, very true," I replied as I finally touched the cuirass. That touch brought back many memories.

"I will leave you," Hap turned away and headed for the stairs.

"Hap, thank you."

"No need, brother. I will always be there for you. Otherwise, mother and father would fatten my lip if they were still alive," Hap finally turned and left me alone.

I slowly peeled the pieces of armor away from the stand, allowing me to get at the gambeson. Over the years, I learned to don my armor without the aid of another. My fingers did not take long to remember how to buckle everything in its place. Finally, after donning my armor, I looked at the two swords lying at the base; one, like most of the swords used by my people, was a two-handed battle sword that stood about six feet, and the other was like that of a bastard blade one that could be wielded either one-handed or two-handed. I grabbed my sword belt and strapped it on, followed by the bastard sword. Before I grabbed my battle sword, I drew my other sword and traced my hand over the edge, along the blood channel, and traced over the engraved words: *Blood and death is life anew.* It was a saying that Ma'yta used to tell me years ago. I returned the blade to its sheath, grabbed my helm and battle sword, and returned to the main floor. Upon entering the kitchen, I found Arawa feeding Syry a bottle of milk, and the sight brought me back to when I had returned home once to my Ma'yta nursing our youngest E'yti. Seeing Arawa feeding Syry made me realize how much my girls meant to me and that I would have done anything for them.

Arawa did not say anything when I came from below as she continued to feed Syry, slowly swaying from side to side while humming an old tune of our people. I saw that young Tee, their elven helper, was helping to prepare breakfast, and from time to time, Arawa would make subtle remarks about how to do something or to add something.

"Simple eggs and ham for breakfast unless you want something else, A'kull?" asked Arawa.

"Eggs and ham will be fine, thank you," I replied as I rested my battle sword and helm against the wall near the doorway between the forge room and the kitchen. As I sat at the table, young Tee placed a plate of food before me. "Thank you, Tee," I ate quickly and gathered the last of my gear before I took Syry from Arawa.

"Take care of her, A'kull," stated Arawa before I kissed her cheek and walked out of the kitchen, gathering my battle sword and helm.

Chapter 5

A Snow Mount

As I left the kitchen and entered the forge room, I found Ochui, T'hetha, and Sewa waiting for me. I paused momentarily, looked down into Syry's eyes, and thought to myself. For the first time in sixty years, I had a reason to live and a reason to fight, for I felt that Syry was destined for far more than I could ever dream of.

"A'kull, are you ready?" Ochui asked me as I looked at Syry.

"Yes, I am. Just one stop before we leave the city," I replied.

"Lead the way," then, with a nod to Ochui, I walked to Hap and hugged him.

"Farewell, brother, until we see each other again," Hap said as we embraced.

"Death and honor, brother," I replied as we touched foreheads and ended our embrace. Then, without waiting for a reply, I headed for the shop door where Sewa was holding the door.

As we stepped out, the assault of the morning sun was a bit unnormal, for usually there was always some cloud cover whether they brought rain or not. However, just as Ochui exited Hap's shop, Tah'kainn and Da'kian came jogging out of trying to catch up with us.

"Tah'kainn and Da'kian, it has been too long. What are you doing here?"

"It has been too long, Ochui. We came into town last night, and at first, we were passing through been, then we found A'kull here last night and decided to travel with him," replied Tah'kainn.

"Well, two more swords and even better company would be welcomed. Where are your mounts?"

"Thanks, we will be glad to join you. Our horses are at the stables just outside of town."

With a simple nod from Ochui, Tah'kainn, and Da'kian fell in beside him, following close behind Syry and myself, while T'hetha walked in the front and Sewa walked beside me. Ochui was also leading their horses. As we neared the town square, it felt like every eye was upon us, for rarely were we ever in such numbers together in such a public setting, but no matter, we pushed on.

"A'kull, where is the shop you needed to stop by?" asked T'hetha.

"Take the next left; it will be a few doors down," I replied. T'hetha turned down the street I had told her of; shortly after that, we came to the tailor shop Silken Seam of Tina and Hal. I entered the shop the same as before and was greeted by Hal as he arranged already-made shirts on the counter.

"A'kull, welcome again. Tina has your order in the back. You can go ahead and go through," Hal greeted me and gestured to the curtain over the doorway leading to the back of their shop.

"A'kull, welcome. Here is your order: six outfits for her, a dozen changing clothes, and a small blanket made of fox fur and backed with Elven silk," stated Tina.

"I did not ask for the last," I replied.

"No, you did not, but I figured it would be handy in keeping her warm during your travels," as Tina finished speaking, I pulled a small gold bar from my coin pouch and placed it in her hand. "This is far too much, A'kull."

"Maybe, but take it as a gesture of goodwill and thanks for concealing the truth of who you have seen."

"Very well, then, thank you. While I do not practice my art much anymore, if you ever need help, please do not hesitate to ask. Ella was a beautiful friend, and I will mourn her daily, but seeing her daughter gives me pride in knowing that part of her is still alive in this world," with a curt nod, I grabbed the bundle of items that Tina had prepared for me. I walked out, giving a slight wave of goodbye as I passed Hal, who was still working. As I came out, my companions were on edge as if expecting trouble.

"What is it, Ochui?" I asked in a low voice as I came up behind him.

"We have drawn too much attention to ourselves. If you are done, we need to leave," he replied.

I nodded yes to Ochui and, with a nod, returned to the others; we started heading to the main gate. As we entered the edge of the town square, the usual clamor of noise suddenly stopped as a group of guards opposite shouted at us to stop where we were. Ochui, Tah'kainn, and Da'kian came up alongside T'hetha, with all of them resting their hands on the handles of their swords, ready to draw and fight, a fight I hoped would not happen. The crowd moved out of the way as the guards approached us; simultaneously, a smaller group of five came up behind us. As they neared, I slid my helm on, freeing my right hand while my left still carried my battle sword. Just as the leading group of guards approached, Ochui called out.

"We do not want any trouble. Let us leave, and we will go peacefully!" he shouted.

"I do not see any trouble as we outnumber you three-to-one," stated the lead guard.

While they may have outnumbered us, they would not have survived a fight against us. Our height and strength allowed us to fight at the power of fifteen to twenty men, which only an Orc or a goblin could nearly match in combat. As the guards approached, they drew their weapons, but none moved to attack.

"You are carrying a baby with you, and we need to see if it is an elf or not," commanded the lead guard.

Ochui took a single step forward before he replied. At the same time, he drew his sword and rested the point on the ground, his hands resting upon the pommel.

"If you want to find out if the baby is an elf or not, you will pay for it with your lives; I guarantee that even outnumbered. Now shall we begin the dance of death, or shall you move from our path and keep your pathetic little lives?" Replied Ochui as he stood in between our group and the group of soldiers

"You cannot beat all of us, fool; in the end, we will win. Shows us whether that baby is an elf or not, and we can end this matter," retorted the guard.

"What if the baby is human? Hmm?" asked Ochui.

"Simple, you can leave; if not, then a fight," replied the guard.

"Well, it will be a fight because it is no one's business whether the baby is an elf or not," stated Ochui.

As Ochui finished speaking, every guard raised their weapons to a fighting posture; however, their move was wasted.

"SERGEANT! You and your men will sheath your weapons at once!" shouted a man sitting on horseback at the edge of the town square surrounded by a dozen guards.

"Sire, that baby may be an elf, and there is a price on the head of an elf baby out of Sitthi...."

Before the sergeant could finish speaking, his lord replied. "A bounty from Sitthi means nothing to me or my lands. NOW! Sheath those weapons," commanded the lord.

The guards did as they were commanded, and they stepped back. As the lord rode towards us, Ochui sheathed his blade.

"Thank you, Lord?"

"Lord Toran of Clan Hanen," Lord Toran stayed in his saddle as he talked with Ochui, who only had to look up slightly as his head was just below Lord Toran's collarbone.

"Thank you, Lord Toran. If there is nothing else, we should be going," stated Ochui.

"I will not ask you your name or what you are doing in my city, but heed this. Koyla lost his most prized hostage not long ago, the former elven queen and her child. While I hold no allegiance with Koyla, I would not protect anyone running from him either," stated Lord Toran.

"All the more reason for us to depart so no one can begin to question us or you, Lord Toran," replied Ochui.

"Be on your way then."

Lord Toran and his men moved off, allowing us to leave the city and meet with the rest of our party at the stables.

As we approached the stables outside of Kent, we found Unka, Vah'tial, and Ankou waiting for our arrival, with all their horses ready to go. All the horses were of heavy build, and my people were much bigger than humans. Ochui, Sewa, and T'hetha took to their mounts as Vah'tial handed me the reins to an all-white female Shire. She nickered as I took the reins, making me slowly stroke her head and neck.

The stable owner came out from the barn and walked over to us. "She is a handful, a former war horse. No one has ever managed to stay seated on her," stated the stable owner.

"I am guessing that her owner died in battle?" I asked, looking back over my shoulder as I stroked her head.

"Yes, although I do not know who her owner was," replied the stable owner.

"Does she have a name?" I asked.

"No, I have never named her for how much a pain she is."

I did not even reply to the stable owner on his last remark. Instead, I slowly ran my hands around her neck and body, checking her tack and ensuring everything was well. As I did this, I did find a few scars blurred into her white coat. While I looked everything over, Tah'kainn and Da'kian gathered their horses. After checking everything, I took the saddle's horn in hand and my foot in the stirrup and swung up onto her back. As I settled into the saddle, she twitched ever so slightly, almost warning me that she did not want me on her back.

"Easy, girl," I spoke softly, stroking her shoulder.

"Ready to go, A'kull?" asked Ochui.

With a nod to him, he reined his horse over and started in front, leading our small company. As we rode on throughout the day, everyone had their eyes scanning the distant horizon, looking for potential threats. Finally, around midday, we stopped at a small stream, letting the horses drink and graze for a bit as we stretched our legs.

"Ochui, where are we headed to?" asked Unka.

"To the elven village of Ta'neek. We should be able to get a ship there that is headed," replied Ochui and asked. "Where do you want to take her, A'kull?"

"Home to Bliźniacy," I replied.

"Home it is then," stated Ochui.

Bliźniacy(The Twins) are two mountains, Śnieżna Góra Kruka (Snow Raven Mountain) and Góra Ryś Śnieżny (Snow Lynx Mountain), that lay in the far western region of Ellrifold. Of the two mountains, the northern one, Śnieżna Góra Kruka, was considered by most of my people to be our home. So, after our short break, we mounted again and rode on until the sun started setting in the west. This became our routine for the next six days until we reached Ta'neek.

Chapter 6

For a Ship Home

After six days of riding from dawn to dusk, we finally arrived at the elven village of Ta'neek. The town lived on raising sheep for wool and meat and trading elven goods from nearby clans that did not want to deal with people other than their own. We arrived just after nightfall. For the most part, the village was quiet, with only a handful of lanterns lit. However, as we moved further into the village, we found that the trade building, which also served as the inn, was bustling with life and music. As we reined up in front of the trade building, a young boy swept the wooden walkway and ignored us as we dismounted.

"Boy, is there a stable nearby?" asked Ochui as he dismounted. The boy did not reply but instead pointed to the corner. "Around the corner?" Asked Ochui, and the boy nodded in return.

Ochui walked his horse around the corner, heading in the direction the boy pointed to, with us following him. The stables were massive for the number of stalls, the open fence area for horses, and the number of wagons inside the stable and out in front. As we came up to the stables, we were greeted by the stable master.

"Evening, need boarding for nine?" asked the stable master.

"Yes," replied Ochui.

"Do you want them individually stalled, or is the turnout fine?"

"The turnout is fine. How much?" Ochui stated and asked.

"One pound for all," replied the stable master.

Before Ochui could dig into his coin purse, I tossed a gold coin to the stable master. We then dismounted and entered the trade building, where one of the servers greeted us while carrying a tray of empty mugs.

"Evening. Find a seat wherever you can, and I will be with you in a moment." Ochui nodded as he led the way farther into the room full of pipe smoke, the smell of ale, wine, and other various odors. Finally, we found the far back corner to be empty and large enough for us to sit. Before we could sit down, I felt a sharp tap on the shoulder, which made me turn around, and in surprise, I found a welcoming face and an old friend.

"A'kull, I thought that was you I saw entering."

"Arma, it has been too long," I replied as I hugged Arma. For a moment, I had forgotten about Syry, who was in the sling under my cloak and promptly kicked Arma when we squished her.

"Ow, what?" Arma pulled back my cloak, revealing Syry. "Who is this little darling?" asked Arma.

As I pulled Syry from the sling, I replied. "She is the daughter of Ella and Danu."

"A'kull!" Unka shouted at me as if I had made an error.

"Unka, we are surrounded by elven people who would never dare turn us aside," I retorted.

"We had heard of Ella's recent escape and possible death, but we feared for her child as well," stated Arma.

"Thankfully, no, she is not," I replied.

Our conversation had drawn many people over to us, and many started asking if she was the daughter of Ella and Danu. I answered yes many times, and then finally, an elven warrior who stood nearly seven foot, with his brown hair cut short, which made his ears stand out, but the scar over his right eye was what drew my attention the most; banged on the bell near the bar getting everyone's attention.

"SILENCE! Silence," he shouted. Finally, all the talk and noise stopped. As he approached, he gestured to us and asked. "Arma, who is this, and who are they?"

"I am A'kull; this is Sewa, Ochui, Tah'kainn, Unka, Vah'tial, T'hetha, Ankou, and Da'kian," I replied and gestured to each as I called their names out.

"Welcome to Ta'neek; I am Gaeleath and commander of the village guard," stated Gaeleath. "Is it true that this young child is the daughter of King Danu and Queen Ella?" he asked.

"She is indeed the daughter of Danu and Ella," I replied.

This time, everyone heard me, and there were numerous gasps and cries from what they heard. Many also bowed their heads in silence and respect.

"I think I can speak for everyone here. You are welcome here, and no one here will turn their back on you," stated Gaeleath.

"Thank you, Gaeleath," I replied and asked. "Who can we speak with about rooms?" Gaeleath gestured at Arma. "You?" I asked surprisingly.

"Yep, me, A'kull. I own the place. I have rooms available for all of you," replied Arma

"Thank you, Arma."

"Of course, old friend. Food, drink, name it, and I will bring it to you," stated Arma.

We all ordered something to eat and drink while Arma and I talked. Shortly after that, our food and drink were brought to us. As we were eating, Gaeleath came over to us.

"What brings you here?" asked Gaeleath.

"Looking for a ship that can take us to Na Cúpla," I replied.

"That should be easy. I will help you find a ship in the morning," remarked Gaeleath.

"Thank you, Gaeleath," Ochui responded before I could. "What have you heard regarding Ella and her child?" asked Ochui.

"Not much other than Ella escaping, but feared dead, the same for her child. Koyla's men have molested some of our traders as they look for them," replied Gaeleath.

"Any come to harm from it?" asked Ochui.

"No, mostly just roughed up, but no killing. I will leave you to your meals and beds and meet you in the morning."

"Thank you," I replied to Gaeleath, who nodded in return as he stood up, leaving us in peace for the remainder of the night.

As the night wore on, the people went home, and we made our way up the rooms Arma had prepared for us. Almost all of us had room to ourselves, but I did ask Sewa to stay with me, for she was also family, being the youngest sister of my late wife, Ma'yta. She did not object to my request. Come morning, Gaeleath was true to his word in helping us find a ship that would take us where we wanted to go, including our horses. After leaving Ta'neek, surprisingly, our ship made no stops along the way to do trading but instead headed for the closest port he could sail into to deliver us to our destination. Ochui asked him about this, and the captain replied that he wanted to ensure that the child would be safe from the clutches of Koyla, and the best way to do this was to get her as far away as possible. So after eight days on the water, we made it to Dunnagall on the western shore of Ellrifold and the western side of the great elven and dwarven city Valhalla, which lies just northeast of Śnieżna Góra Kruka.

Chapter 7

Loyalty and Protection

At times, I find it hard to think back all those years ago when I first brought Syry to Śnieżna Góra Kruka (Snow Raven Mountain) and the years that followed. During the first twenty years at Śnieżna Góra Kruka, I saw her grow from a baby into a beautiful young woman who had mastered everything thrown at her. From fighting with weapons to the arcane magic of our world. More importantly, though, she harnessed a power I had never seen before. That power allowed her to vanish from sight only to turn up beside you without making a sound, let alone you being aware of it. In time, this power became her greatest weapon. Throughout those years, I told her the stories of her people and her parents. By the time she was twenty-five, her anger and hatred for Koyla had made her reckless during her training, but it also taught her a powerful lesson: to vanish, she needed to keep herself calm and focused. Over the next five years, her hatred calmed, for she fell in love with another elf, but some never agreed with the choice for her passion, which was Lyra, another woman around the same age.

Sitting here writing her story and being reminded of another part of her tale is funny as I look at my silver raven skull hanging on the wall overlooking my desk and my writings. Just after she turned sixteen, she found an injured white raven fledgling near the top of Śnieżna Góra Kruka.

In time, she raised it from the fledgling that it was to a beautiful, fully grown raven that never left her side. However, what drew my attention the most was that its eyes were not the normal yellow-green like most of its kind; instead, they were a deep royal sapphire blue.

Excuse my rambling; my mind is not what it once was. Shortly after Syry and Lyra turned thirty, they went through the bonding or marriage right. Many called them fools and saw no sense in their bonding, for a child would never be, but it did not stop them. Instead, it made them fight for each other's love evermore. Then, a few years later, Syry's fate changed, for a visitor came to Snow Raven Mountain; it was early spring morning when a battered and heavily scarred elf came a calling.

"Welcome, stranger; what brings you here?" asked Hua'suiiln as he opened the entrance gate of the mountain.

Instead of replying, the elf asked in an almost heavy, rasping breath as he entered the mountain. "I am looking for the fallen Princess?"

"Follow me," stated Hua'suiiln. Who then led the man to our common hall just down from the gate. "Wait here; have a seat and some water or wine," Hua'suiiln commanded and offered the elf as he sat at one of the nearby tables. Hua'suiiln then left the common hall to find me in our home's upper levels. "A'kull, a visitor is looking for Syry," he informed me as I fletched new arrows.

"Who is he?" I asked.

"An elf who is old and who has seen harsh times. He is in the hall waiting for you."

"Thank You, Hau'suiiln. I will see to him," I replied as Hua'suiiln left my chamber.

I left my chambers and headed for the common hall a moment later. When I entered the common hall, I found this elf sitting at a table sipping a cup of wine. "Welcome, friend. I am A'kull," I greeted and introduced myself. "How can I assist you?" I asked.

The man looked over at me, almost confused, before he replied. "You cannot. I am looking for the fallen Princess," he stated as I approached him.

"Before I let you see her, I need to know who you are and why you want to see her?" I asked.

"Sorry, I am Conri. I once served King Danu and Queen Ella. Over the years, there have been whispers that the Princess is alive and well in the West. I am here because Koyla has lost his grip over his lands, and many want to fight. Many will not unless they have a leader they can believe in, and I believe that leader to be the fallen Princess, for many are still very loyal to the family," replied Conri.

"Conri, you have suffered from Koyla's iron grip," I stated as I gestured to his left hand where the middle and the ring finger were stubs.

"Yes, I have," Conri replied. "Can you help me find the Princess?" he asked.

"Wait here; I will return shortly," I commanded.

Without waiting for an answer, I left the common hall and went up to Syry's and Lyra's chamber. Thinking back, I regretted knocking on that door at that moment. As I neared their chamber, I could hear them and their laughter. I hesitated to knock for a moment, for I did not think she was ready to face someone from her past but more that it was her parent's past. Finally, I knocked on the chamber door, and Syry answered from within.

"It is open," she answered. I opened the door and walked through to find Lyra on their bed with an elven silk sheet covering her, but Syry, on the other hand, was pouring herself a goblet of wine, standing with only the hair on her head covering part of her chest.

"Seriously, Syry put something on when you welcome someone into your chambers," I informed her as I tried to avoid her nakedness.

"Father, I do not care if other people see me like this," she replied as she gestured to her naked body.

"There is someone here asking for you," I stated, averting my eyes.

"Who?" Syry asked.

"Someone loyal to your parents. I will wait for you outside," without waiting for a reply, I turned and left her chambers, allowing her to dress.

Shortly after that, she joined me as we descended the stairs leading back to the common hall. As we entered the hall, Conri rose and bowed and then kneeled.

"Syry, this is Conri," I stated as I introduced her while she took a few steps toward him.

Without looking up, he replied. "Greetings, Princess. You are a striking resemblance to your mother."

"You knew my parents?" Syry asked.

"Yes, Princess, I knew them; I served in the army, loyal to your family."

"Please rise and sit." She waited a moment before she continued. "What brings you here in search of me?" asked Syry as Conri returned to the stool he had previously occupied.

"Princess, I know you may not care or may not be able to help, but there are hundreds if not thousands of us who are enslaved under Koyla who want to rise against him. Unfortunately, many of our people will not unless they have a leader they can follow," stated Conri.

"And you think that I am that leader?" asked Syry.

"Yes. Our people would follow you to the ancestor gates if needed. It is your place to sit on your parent's throne. Will you pick up the torch to lead your people to freedom?"

Syry did not respond for some time as she weighed what lay before her. "You are asking a lot of me. I do not have an army, and while I know some would easily follow me, it will not be enough. There is also the lack of weapons."

"Princess, an army is waiting for you. All you have to do is lead them. As for the weapons, I know of a cache that was sealed shortly before the fall of your parents, and I know where it is."

"How many are free enough to fight?" Syry asked.

"Not many. Most are enslaved, but at the iron mine not far from Totia, there are over a thousand of your people and are only guarded by less than a hundred," replied Conri.

"How is this possible? Surely, the many would rise against the guards?" I asked Conri.

"The guards keep their children separately locked up, which keeps any from fighting back," replied Conri.

Syry turned towards me, pondering for a moment, and asked. "Father, do you think what he is saying is possible?"

"If we could free the children first, it would eliminate their fear of their children being harmed," I replied. "However, a war will not be easy, and many more will die, but do you want vengeance for your parents and your people?" I asked.

Syry replied and asked. "You know I do, Father. But, Conri, are any of our people free enough to aid us?"

"I have heard rumors of renegades living in the mountains, but I am unsure where," he replied.

"It is a start, Syry. I know some of my people would gladly aid you. Others will also aid you. But do you feel ready to start your next path? A path to war and possibly death?" I replied and asked.

Syry did not respond for some time as she weighed the question and the potential consequences of the actions.

"I am ready, Father."

"Very well. Conri, I will find a room for you to rest." I stated before turning to Syry. "Syry, you owe it to Lyra to tell her of your plans," Syry simply nodded and left.

"A'kull, thank you for the offer of a room, but I will go to Ardara; I have kin there, and I might be able to convince some of them to help her," replied Conri.

"Very well, we will meet in three days in Ardara." Ardara lies near the base of Góra Ryś Śnieżny (Snow lynx mountain).

After escorting Conri out of Śnieżna Góra Kruka, I talked to several of my people about the future Syry was about to undertake. To my surprise, twenty of my people offered to fight for Syry, and several others offered to seek out further aid. After talking with many of my people, I went to the top level and sought out Mi'jei, one of our master armorers. As I suspected, she was working at her forge pounding metal.

"Mi'jei?" I said her name as I stood before her anvil, trying to get her attention.

"A'kull, what can I do for you?" Mi'jei asked as she finished her pounding and put her work back into the coals of her forge, allowing it to reheat.

"Is the armor finished?" I asked.

"Yes, it is," she replied before asking. "I am guessing she will need it?"

"Yes. It seems the ancestors have said it is time for her to take her place on her parent's throne." I replied.

Mi'jei put down her hammer and walked over to a tall oak-built armoire, where she opened it, revealing the armor that I had her make for Syry.

"It is made of pure trinthi'ium, as you asked. It will protect her far better than any other armor," Mi'jei spoke as I looked everything over.

"Thank you, Mi'jei. It is everything I thought it would be. I will present it to her in a day or two."

"It will be here waiting for her. I believe that No'jouit is almost done with the sword."

"Thank you, Mi'jei; I will talk with him," after closing the armoire and Mi'jei returning to her work, I went to the other side of the forge room where No'jouit was working. "No'jouit, is the sword finished?" I asked him as he placed his work in the quenching bath beside his anvil.

He waited for a few moments before answering me. "Almost. Here, take a look," No'jouit pulled his work from the bath, wiped the blade down, and handed me the blade. Unlike my blades of Valhalla steel, this one was made of pure trinthi'ium, making it far lighter than mine. After looking it over, I handed the blade back to No'jouit. "I will have it finished tonight. Before you go, pick through the gems on my table and select the ones you want for the eyes of the raven's head."

I did as No'jouit wanted. After looking over the gems, I selected four sapphires and replied. "These will work. I will leave them here."

"Very good, A'kull. I will have it finished soon."

I turned and left without saying a further word, and instead of going to find Syry, I returned to my chambers and looked over my weapons and armor. For the next few days, Syry trained harder than before, and I connected with various people who offered aid in every way possible.

Chapter 8

Protection from War

Three days had passed since Conri first visited Syry, and the first morning following the three days, I asked Syry to join me in the forge room of Snow Raven Mountain. Shortly after her morning meal, Syry walked into the forge room wearing her usual attire of black-dyed leather pants and a blue elven silk shirt with a tooth of a hakari (Stonefeather Cat) hanging from a silk choker. As she entered the forge room, I saw her eyes darting about the room, trying to figure out why I had asked her to join me in the forge room. Then, Lyra came behind her with Syry's white raven Morna perched on her shoulder. As she approached, I stayed in front of the armoire that held both the armor and the sword that I had requested to be made for her.

"Father, why did you ask me here?" Syry asked me as she stood in front of me.

"A few years ago, I began working with Mi'jei to design and have a suit of armor like no other to be made for you, just as I had asked No'jouit to fashion a blade for you," before she could say anything, I turned around. I opened the armoire doors, revealing the armor and the sword hanging on one of the doors with the belt on the opposite door.

"Father, I already have armor and a sword," Syry stated.

"True, but unlike the hardened leather and mail armor you currently wear, this armor and sword are made of pure trinthi'ium. As a result, the armor will protect you like nothing else, and the sword will hold against anything it can strike," I replied as I moved aside, allowing her to see and approach the armor and the sword. Once she reached the armoire, she slowly traced her hand over the Raven skull, eating the blade from the cross tree. She did likewise with the armor.

"Father, why did you have these made?" Syry asked.

"Because I wanted to ensure you have the best armor and sword possible to ensure your survival," I replied.

"Thank you, father. Did you know that Conri was coming? Is that the reason why you had these made?" she asked.

For a moment, I stayed silent as I did not want to admit that I knew this day would come when she would pick up the fallen torch and take the fight to Koyla to avenge her parents' deaths.

"Syry, I have known for some time that you would want to avenge your parents' deaths. It was just a matter of time. I will leave you to don the armor," as I was about to leave, Syry stopped me with a hug.

"No, please stay and help me."

"Very well," so I stayed with Lyra, who assisted me in helping Syry into the armor. After a few moments, we had finished buckling everything in place, with only her helmet left to don and her sword to hang upon its belt. I pulled the sword from the pegs and offered the blade to Syry, who then pulled the blade free, revealing the phrase: *Shadows Ghost in Blood and Honor* in Elvish script inscription.

"Shadows ghost in blood and honor. A fitting remark, Syry." Lyra stated as she stood just behind her.

"Thank you, Father," Syry stated after she sheathed the sword, which Lyra then hung on the sword belt around Syry's waist.

"When you are ready, Syry, I will meet you in the common hall," without saying a word, Syry hugged me and almost began to weep as we embraced. Just before she let go of me, I kissed her head.

After leaving the forge room, I returned to my chambers and donned my armor. Once I was finished donning my armor, I headed for the common hall. Where, I found: Da'kaalth, Ochui, Sewa, T'hetha, Unka, Hua'suiiln, Tah'kainn, Te'jo, Vah'Taar, Ya'jea-Bo, Ya'tui, Za'kah, A'dqaar, Ba'ytup, Cedah, Canku, Dahru, G'ka'tu, Gakoal, Kul'seair, waiting for Syry and myself.

Thinking back, I do not believe Syry knew that any of my people would be willing to fight for her. However, I was shocked when Kul'seair, the eldest of my people, came to my chambers the day after Conri had visited Syry and said he would be proud and honored to fight with Syry. I was against it then, for he held so much wisdom of our people and was also our eldest. In time, however, I realized that he wanted the chance to die in battle wearing his armor and sword in hand than to die in a bed. As I stood at the entrance of the common hall and looked at people who were my friends and who many I considered to be family, Syry came up behind me, with Morna perched on her shoulder and Lyra standing behind her in her armor. After a moment's pause, I moved aside, allowing Syry to see everyone who offered their help. Syry was shocked, for she did not see it coming that any of my people were willing to fight for her. Still, as she slowly moved into the room, Kul'seair stepped forward and kneeled in front of Syry, allowing himself to see eye-to-eye for his height towered above her.

In his normal deep barrel, yet soft-spoken voice, he addressed her. "Syry, I have watched you grow, train, and study. You have become another daughter to me. Because of this, it will be my honor to fight beside you and serve in your name. Just remember your training, and you will survive."

"Thank you, Kul'seair, and even more so for fighting beside me," Syry stated as she leaned forward and hugged Kul'seair, who returned her hug.

After that, little more was said between Syry and the others before we made our way outside to overlook the field in front of Śnieżna Góra Kruka. As we exited Śnieżna Góra Kruka, a cheer went up from everyone assembled out front. As we parted away from shielding Syry, she could finally see all those that cheered and called her name, and they numbered nearly two thousand, made chiefly of elves, but there were some dwarves and orcs that rallied to Syry. There were also a few humans who offered to fight. As Syry stood at the foot of granite stairs leaving the mountain, she stared out at everyone gathered, and while I would never call her timid in her ability to fight, she never cared for large gatherings. What surprised me was her taking a step or two down and speaking out loud and proud enough for everyone to hear her.

"I cannot begin to thank every one of you for your willingness to fight with me, but every uthuk-nari, elf, dwarf, orc, and human will have a place in the kingdom that will be taken back," she stated. After a moment of silence, the valley lit up in a roar of approval, with many shouting their own clan's words or shouting only victory and death now await.

Many of my people came to say their goodbyes to us; many knew that the possibility of returning home might not happen. Many tried in these last moments to plead with many of my kin to stay, but for those of us who stood by Syry, our hearts and minds had already been made up. For me, Syry was the only family I had left, yes I had my brother Ha'thap and his wife Arawa, who were still alive, and Sewa, my wife's sister, who was there for me as well, the only one that I cared for was Syry, and it meant a great deal to me to see her take the step to avenge her parents' death.

Chapter 9

An Oath Sworn

It took us nearly a fortnight to reach the shores just north of Ta'neek from the cove just north of Snow Raven Mountain. We finally reached the shores north of Ta'neek on the 20th of Feall (August) 1246. Once we landed, many of the leaders of the various groups sent out their people to gather further supplies while the leaders and Syry discussed the next steps and how to proceed going north. Some wanted to strike hard and fast at Koyla sitting in Sitthi, but many argued that we needed to push north but do it at a pace that allowed us time to gather and build up the army. Ultimately, the second option of moving north and collecting more numbers was the chosen course of action.

Nearly a month had passed since making land north of Ta'neek when we encountered our first battle that marked the official beginning of the Vengeance War, as it came to be called. That first battle was small and quick, with only a slight loss of fifty lives on our side, while General Dannern, loyal to Koyla, lost over three hundred out of four hundred and fifty. Something still vivid in my mind about the aftermath of that battle that affected the rest of the war was Syry's absolute message that no quarter would be given to any who fought in Koyla's name. This angered many of the humans who fought for Syry, but many also understood why, as Koyla had done the same to the people loyal to her parents and those who had fought for them.

The day after that first battle, while the camps were beginning to awaken from the night, the guards on watch reported a single rider sitting on the hill to the north. Many thought it could be a scout of Koyla's, and while many of the leaders debated what to do, I took to my horse and rode towards this rider, and as I did, the rider stayed. As I rode up, I saw the rider wearing a mix of plate and mail armor and a simple helmet covering most of his face. Yet, even as I reined up, he did not ride off.

"Morning, is there something that you want?" I asked this stranger. Before he spoke, he removed his helm and pulled back the mail coif covering his head, revealing his Elvish ears.

"Do you have a name, uthuk-nari?" he asked.

"A'kull, and what is your name?"

"Ah, the Butcher of Ka'leen Bay, I know the name. Before I give you my name, I want to know if the child of King Danu and Queen Ella is leading this army?" He nodded towards the field behind me.

"She is," I replied.

"Well, then, my name is Laiex Heir'ic. Will you take me to her?" Laiex asked.

"First, tell me why you are here and why you want to speak with her?"

"You protect her?"

"Yes," I retorted. "I am the one that saved her from Koyla's hunters when her mother escaped."

"You care for her as if she was your own," Laiex stated.

"Yes, I do," I replied.

"Very well; I am the rebels' leader and was once a general under her father, King Danu," Laiex replied.

"Is there anyone that can prove your words?" I asked.

"I believe Conri is with the army?"

"He is."

"Go ask him of me, and I will wait until you return."

I did not even reply as I turned my horse back to camp and spurred her forward in a fast trot. I returned to the main tent that served as our meeting area, where all the leaders discussed the next steps. As I returned to the tent, Conri was exiting it, and without dismounting, I asked him.

"Conri, do you know an Elf named Laiex Heir'ic?" I asked.

"Yes, I do," Conri replied. "He was the only general Koyla did not execute, and now he is the rebels' leader," Conri stated.

"Can we trust him, Conri?" I asked.

"Yes, you can. His loyalty is to the crown and the royal family of Totia," Conri replied.

"Te'jo, get your horse and come with me. Where is Syry?"

"Back in her tent with Lyra," stated Vah'Taar, who stood nearby. "Go back to this Laiex, and I will get Syry."

As I turned my horse around, Te'jo retrieved his horse and began to follow me as I left the camp, returning to this Laiex Heir'ic.

"Conri confirms that he does know you, but before I escort you to her. Do you have any weapons?" I asked.

Laiex tossed his weapon belt wrapped around an ax and a long knife without replying.

"This is it?" I asked.

"Yes, I carry nothing else," Laiex replied.

"Follow," I ordered as I turned my horse back, and Laiex followed me while Te'jo brought up the rear.

As we returned to the tent, the rest of my people had formed up in front, with Syry standing between Sewa and Kul'seair and Lyra standing just behind her. My people were on edge as no one knew if we could trust this Laiex Heir'ic. As we reined up and dismounted, I handed off my mare to an elf attendant who also took Laiex's and Te'jo's horses. While I did not take my place in line with my people, I did stay between Syry and Laiex, who immediately kneeled in front of Syry.

"My Queen, I am Laiex Heir'ic. I served your father and your mother and will serve you until my death and the ancestors take me from this land," Laiex stated.

"I am no queen Laiex. That title was taken when Koyla took my father's head and crown," Syry replied.

"Maybe not in the title, my Queen, but in name, yes. You are the rightful ruler of Totia. As for the crown, I can provide that, and just as well, I can provide more troops for your cause, my Queen."

"You have the king's crown?" I asked as Laiex was still kneeling.

"Yes, I do. Koyla tossed it away after the beheading, and I retrieved it when I escaped the iron mine in the north," Laiex replied.

"Rise, Laiex," Syry ordered.

"I will not rise until I have sworn myself to you, my Queen, and in your name."

"Syry is my name."

"My Queen Syry, in your name and the name of your family, I swear myself to you, to your life, and only upon death will my vow of service be lifted."

Syry stepped forward and offered her hand to Laiex, which he accepted and lightly kissed.

"Rise, Laiex," Syry commanded.

"Thank you, my Queen."

"You said you have the crown of my father?" Syry asked.

"Yes, it is at my camp in the ruins of Totia," Laiex replied.

"Will you take me to Totia and the crown?" Syry asked.

"Yes, my Queen. It will only take us several days to reach Totia from here," Laiex replied.

"We will leave shortly then," Syry ordered.

"Syry, what of our plans for relocating the camp?"

"Elder Lomman, you and the other elders will take the army, move to Lo'karan, and lay siege to it. There, you will wait until I rejoin you," Syry replied.

"Laiex, here are your weapons; sorry for the lack of trust," I stated as I returned Laiex's weapons to him.

"Trust is earned and not given, so a wise choice," Laiex replied.

As we spoke, Syry and Lyra left the group to return to Syry's tent, where they donned their armor. During the few moments that Syry had returned to her tent, the remaining of my people gathered their gear and horses. Once Syry and Lyra had donned their armor, they mounted their horses waiting outside the tent and reined up in front of the main tent.

"My Queen, I was not expecting to see you in armor," Laiex stated, almost stumbling over his words as he addressed Syry.

"I will not sit idle as others fight this war," Syry stated as she looked upon Laiex.

Laiex retorted. "Who am I to argue with, my Queen," Syry nodded in return at Laiex's statement.

After a moment, the rest of my people reined up, with only myself and Laiex still unmounted, which did not last long. As we left the camp, almost everyone lined the path leaving camp and kneeled in recognition of Syry as Queen. Only Da'kaalth, Canku, Gakoal, and Za'kah remained with the army as the rest of us went with Syry.

Chapter 10

The Crown

After leaving camp, it took us only nine days to reach Totia, where we found more than five hundred Elven warriors who all served and fought alongside Laiex. As we entered the ruins of Totia, these warriors kneeled and shouted, "Long live the Queen." For a moment, Syry looked at the sea of warriors and wondered how people who were so proud and loyal could be defeated, and when she asked this question, not one of us could provide an answer.

"Laiex, how many warriors are present?" Syry asked him as he reined up alongside her.

"At the moment, five hundred, but probably another hundred and fifty are not here," Laiex replied.

Without replying, Syry dismounted and began to walk through the kneeling warriors.

"Laiex, were you here the day that my father was murdered?" Syry asked.

"Yes, I was," Laiex replied.

"Show me where it happened," Syry commanded.

Laiex dismounted his horse with a nod and escorted Syry to where her father had been killed. As they neared the spot, Laiex stayed back, and Syry continued forward. Even after all the years had passed, the ground was still stained with her father's blood. Once at the spot, Syry dropped to her knees and lowered her chin to her chest. All of us were silent and giving her the space she needed. I later learned what came to follow that moment.

"At that moment, I saw my parents and other kin, all looking at me and speaking in one voice. Syry, you will have your vengeance, not just for your us, but for the many that have suffered at the hand of Koyla....." She told me all of this and more after we left Totia. Even as she told me this, I felt that there was something else that she had not mentioned, and with some pressure, I got her to tell me what she was afraid of speaking about. The only figure that she knew was that of Lyra or at least somebody who looked like her. After telling me this, she asked me what it might mean. I told her that the ancestors were the only ones who knew the true meaning of this, but it also might have been their way of gaining your trust by showing her someone who she trusted more than anything else.

That first night there in Totia, there were many fires and meals, and Syry took her time mingling with almost everyone there. Lyra and a few of us were never far from her as she did this. However, when she asked about her father's crown, Laiex told her to wait until morning, and when she pressed him more, he kept saying to wait until morning. This alone gave me and others of my people great concern, making us ponder if this was nothing more than a trap. Come morning, these worries proved untrue. Finally, just as the sun was breaking the top of the trees, Laiex went to the ruined building Syry and Lyra shared and asked her and those who wanted to were to follow him.

Many of the buildings were still in ruin from when Koyla attacked, but none of these buildings were of no concern to us as Laiex led us a short way from the central clearing of Totia. After our brief walk, we stopped in front of a low hill on the outskirts of the ruined city; at first glance, it looked just a simple hill, but Laiex proved that untrue as he pulled aside a curtain that blended into the hillside.

"My Queen, please follow me inside. There is someone you need to speak with, and they can provide you with the answers you seek," Laiex commanded.

"Laiex, my patience is running thin; tell us who and why she needs to go in," I demanded.

"A'kull, if you mistrust me that much, then go first," Laiex replied.

Without replying and denying Syry the chance to object, I bent forward and ducked as I came through the passage. It took my eyes a moment to adjust to the lack of light, for only a handful of candles were burning around the room. Once my eyes had changed, I found someone I thought to be long dead.

"Meesha'ka, I cannot believe it is you after all these years and that you are alive," I said as I kneeled before her and looked into her royal purple eyes.

"A'kull, it has been too long. Where have you been all these years?" she stroked my face like a mother soothing her child as she spoke.

"That is a long story, Meesha'ka, and I will tell you in time. But as to why I am here. Syry! Come!" I replied.

As Syry and Lyra entered the chamber, they let their eyes adjust as Syry asked. "Father, is everything alright?"

"Yes, come over here," I replied.

Syry looked towards me and started to approach. She stopped just a short step from my heel, and Meesha'ka rose from her chair when she stopped.

"Welcome, child, you are indeed your mother's child. I can see her in you. What a beauty have you grown into, "Meesha'ka stated. "Who is this?" asked Meesha'ka as she gestured to Lyra, who was coming up behind Syry.

"Who are you?" Syry asked before she answered Meesha'ka's question.

"Forgive me, child. My name is Meesha'ka. I knew your parents when both were no taller than my knee," Meesha'ka replied.

"To answer your question, Meesha'ka, this is Lyra, my mate, my love, and whatever else you may want to call our relationship, our affection," Syry replied as Lyra moved just behind her and lightly placed her hand on Syry's waist.

"A beautiful match," stated Meesha'ka and asked. "Have you come here seeking your father's crown? Yes?"

"Correct," Syry replied.

"Then please sit. Laiex, bring the chest," commanded Meesha'ka. While I was kneeling and Syry and Lyra were entering, I had not seen Laiex enter, but he was not the only one, as Kul'seair had also joined. "Father, you are here?" asked Meesha'ka.

Kul'seair moved around us and embraced his daughter Meesha'ka, whom he had not seen in some time and thought long dead as well. While they embraced, Laiex brought forth a simple oak chest. When Laiex put the chest down between Syry and Meesha'ka, Meesha'ka ended her hug with her father and opened the chest, revealing a beautifully crafted crown made from trinthi'ium and gold studded with six blood diamonds evenly placed around the crown, as it lay on blue velvet. Once the chest was open, Syry stared at the crown as it lay there. "The crown of Totia was made by my people more than six hundred years ago and was gifted to your ancestors, and it is now yours," Meesha'ka stated.

"Thank you, Meesha'ka, and to you, Laiex, for finding it. What now?" Syry stated and asked.

"My Queen, it was my duty as a soldier to your family. So I had to make the crown safe," Laiex replied as he stood near the back of the room.

"Syry, here shortly, we will go to the Grove just north of here, to where your ancestors are buried and where every king and queen of your family has been crowned," Meesha'ka stated.

"Is my father buried there?" Syry asked.

"I am afraid not, Syry. After his death, Koyla left his remains for the carrion, and no one was left, nor were any able to return to give a proper burial," Meesha'la replied.

"I want to find at least his head and bury it with our ancestors," Syry stated.

"My Queen, I am sorry, but there is no way of telling where your father's head was taken or by whom it was taken by," Laiex stated.

"There might be a way," I replied.

"A'kull, you cannot be serious, the Obrzęd Krwi Przodków?!" Meesha'ka questioned and remarked.

"The what?" Syry asked.

"The Rite of Ancestors Blood is where you combine the shavings of a Stoneheart Tree, a small amount of your blood, and the last is the ash of an aeshies. All it is mixed with spirits, and you then drink it."

"It is poison; it will kill her," Stated Laiex and he asked. "No one is ever allowed to use anything related to the Stoneheart Tree unless it has been granted to them."

"The royal marker of Totia was gifted to her family by the ancestors so that it will be the source. As for the rest, yes, there is a risk of death, but I know no other way to find an ancestor's remains. Syry, the choice to take this cocktail is yours alone," I replied.

"Father, are you sure there is no other way?" Syry asked.

"Yes, there is no other way."

"Very well then. How does one obtain an aeshies?" Asked Syry.

"Puisín, please no. I do not want to lose you," Lyra pleaded with Syry. But it was the first time, I saw Syry ignore her. Puisín was the name of affection that Lyra often called Syry; it means kitten in the elvish tongue.

"If my memory recalls, they grow to the west of here," I stated as I looked into Lyra's eyes.

"I believe they still do, A'kull," Meesha'ka replied.

"I will go and find one," I stated.

"Father, I will go with you," Syry stated and asked. "Lyra, I want you to join us," Lyra nodded in response.

"My Queen, I will go as well."

"No, Laiex, you will remain here," Syry ordered.

"But, My…," Laiex pleaded.

"My answer is final," Syry replied.

It was the first time I could recall Syry starting to act like the queen she was meant to be. Without waiting for another remark, I headed for the outside, and like how I entered, I kept my head low as I exited. As my eyes adjusted to the changing brightness, Syry and Lyra came out behind me.

However, before we could step further away, Syry's raven Morna landed before us, holding an aeshies by a petal. Syry was the first to approach. She kneeled in front of Morna and held her hands out; Morna gently placed the flower into Syry's awaiting hands.

"Careful, Syry, you do not want to get any juices from the flower on you," I remarked as she looked back at me, wondering how Morna knew to bring the flower.

"Who is this? A friend, Syry?" Meesha'ka asked, who stood just behind me nearer the entrance to the hill.

"This is Morna. I found her as a fledgling," Syry replied as she stroked the top of Morna's head and as I took the flower from Morna.

"A'kull, I know the aeshies and the blood-salts that come from them are deadly, but I think it would be wise to do this in the Grove and at the base of the Stoneheart Tree," Meesha'la remarked.

"A wise choice, A'kull, especially considering the risk involved," Kul'seair added as he stood beside Meesha'ka.

"Agreed. Do you have the other items needed?" I asked Meesha'ka, who nodded in return. "Then let us go to the Stoneheart Tree and begin this process," I recommended.

Laiex guided us to the Grove and Stoneheart Tree of Totia, lying on the outskirts of the ruined city. As we passed several groups of rebel soldiers, I could hear the whispers of their fears and about what would be happening. I was thankful that none of them chose to follow us, for I was not sure if Syry would survive, and even though I could not see Lyra's eyes, I felt them, for I knew she hated what I had suggested.

Chapter 11

Ancestors Blood

After arriving at the Grove and entering, Meesha'ka and I gathered everything together, burned the aeshies, and began to boil the spirits and shave only a sliver or two from the royal marker that had been with the crown. The flower took a little bit of time to burn completely to ash, and while I watched it burn down, I saw Syry slowly walking among the various markers around the Grove. Every once in a while, Kul'seair would remark about one of the markers. Once the aeshies flower burned down to clear white ash, both Meesha'ka and I finished making the cocktail. After everything was mixed, the ash of aeshies, a shaving sliver of a Stoneheart Tree, and spirits boiled, it needed to cool before we could add the last ingredient, her blood, and then finally, Syry could drink it.

"Syry, it is time," I called out to her as I poured it into a clay cup.

"Now, what, Father?" Syry asked.

"Sit with your back against the Stoneheart Tree, and then let me see your hand," I commanded.

"My hand?" Syry asked.

"There is one last ingredient needed to make this work correctly: the blood of the taker," Meesha'ka remarked.

As Syry sat against the tree, I handed Meesha'ka the potion, cleaned my blade, and prepared a cloth binding.

"Lyra, come and take her other side," I ordered. Lastly, I poured some of the spirits on Syry's hand to help ensure that no infection would set in. "Syry, I have to cut deep enough to get enough to change the color of the mixture. If you would like, another can do this part," I asked.

"No, father, I trust you," Syry replied.

"Very well, this will hurt," I stated.

All Syry did was nod in agreement, and I then proceeded to slice her hand open, allowing her blood to flow freely into the cup. After a few moments, I had enough blood, so I applied the clothing binding to staunch the flow. While I did this, Meesha'ka thoroughly stirred the mixture and returned it to me.

"Syry, this cocktail will cause pain; you must drink the whole thing," I remarked.

"Okay…" Syry stated and sighed.

"Are you ready?" I asked.

"Yes," Syry replied and asked "Is there anything else?"

"Yes. After you drink the cocktail, close your eyes, lean completely against the Stoneheart Tree, and repeat what I say," I replied.

"Okay."

Before Syry took the cocktail from me, she kissed Lyra and promised her that everything would be fine. As Syry took the cocktail from me, Lyra held the hand I had sliced and held onto her as she drank and finally the last of the Rite.

"Blood of my blood, come to me, ancestors of my blood aid me, guide me to my blood. Ancestors hear my call, the blood of my blood hear me, blood by blood, life, and death guide me to those that are lost." Syry repeated after me

without missing a step. As she recounted the lines a second time, Lyra and I continued to hold her. Finally, after a few moments, Syry's head dropped to her chest.

"Puisín!" Lyra shouted as she shook her, fearing she was passing. As she did this, I felt along her neck and found her blood still pumping.

"Lyra, she is alright; the ancestors have her now," I stated.

"Are you sure?" Lyra asked.

"Yes, I am sure; just keep holding her," I replied and Lyra finally stopped shaking her and continued to hold her hand, just as I did.

I do not know how much time had passed since we began the damn rite, but I know it was some time before Syry finally opened her eyes and looked about, allowing herself to regain her awareness and surroundings. Neither Lyra nor I spoke for several moments, but I eventually broke the silence.

"Syry, how are you feeling?" I asked.

"I am okay," Syry replied and stated. "You were not joking about the pain from drinking that," I nodded in agreement.

"Did you see anything?" I asked.

"Yes, it felt like I was seeing through Morna's eyes, but then I realized I was seeing through my fathers, and he led me to where his head should be," Syry replied.

"Good, then the rite was not worthless; was there anything else?" I stated and asked.

"I do not know. Something sounded more like an echo or a whisper than anything."

"Can you describe it?"

"I think so… there was crying, wailing, and then something like the sound of a butcher's hammer hitting meat and then a thud, and the crying became louder and then nothing," stated Syry.

I shook my head while averting her eyes and *whispered, no, I cannot believe this.* Syry, of course, heard this.

"Father, what did you say?" Syry asked.

"Syry, what you heard and saw was something I had hoped would not happen," I replied.

"What would not happen?" Both Syry and Lyra asked this of me.

It took me a few moments before I replied. "What you saw was the death of your father. I hoped you would not experience it, but the Ancestors must have felt that you needed to."

Syry began to weep, which caused Lyra to pull her into her arms, allowing her to bury her head in the nestle of her arms. During this, Syry's hand, which I sliced, slid to Lyra's face, which caused her to pull away and look at the wound.

"What, this cannot be!" Lyra stated.

"Love, what is it?" Syry asked.

"Look, your hand," Lyra replied.

Syry lifted her head, looked to her palm, and saw only a scar, no open wound as it should have been. I took her hand and examined it as well.

"The Ancestors did indeed hear your call," I stated and asked. "Do you feel ready to go and find your father's head?"

Syry nodded yes, so I stood up and helped Syry and Lyra stand. Syry asked that no one else accompany or follow us.

It took us until early evening before we came upon the spot Syry had seen in her vision from the Ancestors. Finally, we found it nestled in the roots of a tree sticking out of a dried stream bed and near a small opening, most likely to a fox or a badger's den. As Syry reached for her father's skull, I expected her to fight some with the roots, for they had grown around the skull, but instead, I saw the roots move away, almost like they were melting away, which stunned Lyra and Syry. Nevertheless, Syry reached for the skull and removed it from the roots. After she had removed it, the roots slid back to where they once had been.

As she held it, I laid a simple black silk cloth on the ground. "Syry, wrap it in this," I recommended and gestured to the cloth on the ground.

After a moment, Syry kneeled, placing her father's skull on the cloth, and slowly wrapped it.

"Come, let us find a place to camp for the night, and come morning, we will return to Totia," I recommended.

Syry then handed me the skull as Lyra helped her up. We then left the stream bed and found a suitable spot for the night. After we found a spot for the night, Syry and Lyra found wood for a fire, and I went to see what food I could hunt for. When I returned with a pair of hares, Syry and Lyra had lit a small fire and were sitting together. After I had returned, I cleaned the hares for cooking as Syry asked me what I knew of her father, if I had ever met him, or if I had met her mother before I found her and Syry together. It was not the first time Syry had asked me of them, but I did not hold back what I knew of them this time. After eating and telling of her parents, I felt I gave her comfort in knowing that they were well-loved by their people and that their love for each other was great. Come morning, we returned to Totia and to crown Syry, burn her father's skull, and bury his ashes before the Stoneheart Tree.

Chapter 12

A Name Cursed

The crowning was not something I could easily forget. As we returned to Totia, every rebel soldier under the command of Laiex was standing at attention and lining the path leading to the Grove and the Stoneheart Tree, where all my people were waiting, along with Meesha'ka and Laiex who was holding a velvet pillow that held the crown. However, before Syry and Lyra came before Meesha'ka and Laiex, they went to the ruined building they had slept in the first night we had spent there. It was not long before Syry and Lyra appeared, now wearing their armor. As they descended the path, Lyra walked one step behind her, holding both of their helms, and Syry's white raven Morna was perched upon her shoulder. As we had waited for them, I had placed her father's skull upon the pyre built before we arrived. Once they had come, they stopped before Meesha'ka.

"Syry, this day has been a long time to come, and it is time, but before I crown you, I must confess something I had hidden from you upon arrival," Meesha'ka remarked.

I knew the secret that Meesha'ka had kept from her, and it was something that I had fought with myself on whether to tell Syry or not, but in the end, it was not my place to say.

"Meesha'ka, what is it?" Syry asked.

"When I told you I knew your mother, it was not a lie, but not the truth. Your mother is of my blood, just as are you...."

"What, how?" Syry asked as she looked at me, but I did not respond.

"Your mother is my sister by both our mother and father," Meesha'ka stated.

"Kul'seair, is she speaking the truth?" Syry asked.

"Yes, she is. I am your mother's father," replied Kul'seair.

"Father, you knew this?" Syry asked.

"Yes, I did," I replied.

"Why did either of you never tell me?" Syry asked, both myself and Kul'seair.

"Syry, it was not my place," I replied.

"Syry, while it was my place to tell you. I was not sure if you were ready to learn it. I am sorry for not telling you," replied Kul'seair.

"I can understand why, and I love you even more than before for your willingness to fight beside me," Syry stated as she looked at both of us.

Kul'seair did not respond; instead he simply nodded.

"Syry, I was also the one that had crowned your father, and I was there when your parents married," Meesha'ka stated.

"Meesha'ka, thank you, and I am honored to have you being the one to do the crowning," Syry replied.

Meesha'ka gestured for Syry to kneel before her so she could begin the crowning.

"The kingdom of Totia may have fallen, but it has not been forgotten by its people and the royal family, who now kneels before the Stoneheart Tree and who is ready to fight to avenge those that have fallen in the name of Totia. Syry, daughter of Danu and Ella, you have come a long way since birth and have returned to your birthright and your people," Meesha'ka stated and asked. "Do you accept the responsibility of being Queen and the duty of Queen in protecting the lives of the people within your borders and avenging the wrongs done to the people and this land?"

"I do. I vow to protect these lands and their people and take vengeance against those who have sought to destroy them," Syry answered.

"By the Ancestors, I Meesha'ka, daughter of Kul'seair and Aurae, sister to your mother Ella. I grant you the title of Queen, and I name you Queen Syry, daughter of Danu and Ella," Meesha'ka placed the Totia crown upon Syry's head. "Rise, Queen Syry."

For a moment, Syry continued to kneel and stayed silent as she weighed what she had just sworn herself to, but finally, she rose and began to address those witnessing this event without turning around.

"I may not have been raised here, nor have I proven myself in battle, but I will take vengeance upon any who have wronged the people of Totia. Lastly, from this day forth, may no one speak his name, for his name is cursed and is just awaiting his!" Before anyone could react, Syry grabbed her dagger, sliced open the hand that I cut for the rite, placed her bleeding hand on the trunk of the Stoneheart, and began to whisper. "Ancestors, hear my words; I curse the name, the man known as Koyla; his life is mine, and if I am to pay with my life to end his, then so be it. So curse his name and take my blood as payment for what I am asking," Syry stated.

Syry pulled away from the tree, leaving a bloodied handprint behind. Even though some of us heard her words, no one was willing to say anything about them to her. Syry then grabbed a nearby burning torch, tossed it on the pyre that held her father's skull, and then walked away as the flames began to eat away at both the wood and the skull. Syry walked to the edge of the Groove and looked upon some six hundred soldiers that had gathered to witness the crowning; before she spoke, she scanned those amassed.

"Rebels, no. Soldiers, you have gathered here to witness my crowning and to put your faith in a leader who is the rightful heir to the Totia throne. While I may be the rightful heir, I do not feel I have earned that right, but I will strive to earn it by fighting beside every one of you. In two days, we will leave the ruins of Totia and march out to meet up with the rest of my forces. Those of you that are leaders, please attend me here on the edge of the Groove," Syry spoke out and ordered.

A mighty cheer went up from every soldier, and some general orders were issued as they dispersed while the leaders approached the Groove. It did not take long for the leaders to present themselves.

"My Queen, let me introduce you to the various leaders of the men and women that are present," Syry nodded in respect to Laiex as he spoke and the leaders began to form. "Cohnal, Hycis, Maith, Sontar, Takari, and Alok. Each command about a hundred, and as for myself, I tended to command over all of them, but that is not always true, for most times we jointly make decisions," stated Laiex.

"Thank you, Laiex, and thank all of you for being here. Before I forget, Conri, Laiex, where are the weapons you mentioned when we first met?" Syry asked of them.

"They are located beneath the city, my Queen. What of the slaves in the iron mine to the north? You did agree to rescue them before much longer," replied Conri.

Syry hesitated momentarily as she looked at everyone gathered around her before asking. "Does anyone know how many are enslaved there?"

"We have never counted all of them, but from what we can figure, there is at least a thousand, maybe more," replied Maith.

"Maith, correct?" Syry asked, and Maith responded in kind. "Let us make that our priority before we meet back up with the rest of my forces. We can make plans on our way up to the mine, so for now, see to getting underway. Conri and Laiex take me to the weapons," Syry commanded.

"Of course, my Queen, follow us," stated Conri.

The rest of the leaders dispersed while Conri and Laiex escorted us to a ruined building and a stairway that took us underground. After a short walk past the stairs, we found a brick wall barring our way. While it was well-built, it would not stop anyone long from getting through.

"Te'jo, A'dqaar, would you care to do the honor?" I asked them, as their weapons were better suited than the rest of ours.

"Syry and everyone else, stand back. This will be quick work," Te'jo commanded as he and A'dqaar hefted their battle axes into position and began to swing their weapons. They had already dislodged a few bricks within their first few hits. From there, the wall came down quickly, and with less than a dozen swings, there was a gap large enough for us to walk through. "Syry after you," Te'jo stated as he swung his ax onto his shoulder.

"My Queen, wait. There should be a trough of oil just past the wall. Let me light a torch and see if it still has oil in it," Laiex stated as he grabbed a torch from the wall sconce, putting steel and flint to it; it quickly grew a flame. As the flame developed, Laiex stepped through the wall and found the trough still holding oil, so he dipped the flaming torch into the oil, causing it to light and spread through the trough that went all the way to the back of the chamber. As the trough lit up, it illuminated row upon row of various weapons and armor.

"Wow, there is more here than I was expecting," Syry stated as she slowly walked down the aisle next to the oil trough.

"Your father was prepared, but sadly, there was not enough time to get all this to those who needed it," Laiex remarked.

"Laiex, gather anybody you need to clear this chamber out. I want everyone properly armed before we move out, and we will take what remains with us," Syry commanded.

"My Queen, that will take some time to make it happen," Laiex remarked.

"Just get it done," ordered Syry as she turned around and walked out, leaving Laiex almost scratching his head, trying to figure out how he would make her orders happen.

I and several others offered to help in the task, and we started by getting everything off the shelves and then placing them in neatly stacked piles outside, where Kul'seair and the rest of the leaders helped in issuing weapons and armor to those who needed them. It was not until nightfall that we completed the task, and at that point, we finally had the chance to rest and eat. During all this, Syry was wondering among the men and women who had taken up the cause of fighting back; while Syry was roving, Totia Lyra was never more than a step away from her. Surprisingly, the camp was ready to leave within the time Syry had ordered, and we started north.

Chapter 13

Freedom and a Child

After leaving Totia, it took us about two and a half days to reach the iron mine in the north. When we arrived within sight of the mine, Syry, Lyra, Kul'seair, Laiex, and myself rode out to the mine, allowing the rest of the army to follow at their slower pace. As we approached, we could hear a lot of yelling coming from the slaves and the guards yelling back, trying to keep control over far superior numbers. However, just before we were within shouting distance, an arrow landed a few feet in front of us, signaling to come no farther, and so we did not, but a lone soldier walked out of the gates barring entrance to the mining camp. None of us dismounted as he came forward, but we could tell he was unarmed as he approached.

"I do not care who you are and why you have come to my doorstep with this rabble, but I would advise you to turn around and leave," stated the lone soldier as he gestured to the army still marching behind us.

"Are you the commander of this mine?" Syry asked loud and clear.

"Yes, I am, and who are you?" the commander replied.

"I am Syry, the Queen of Totia and the rightful ruler of these lands," The man's face and eyes lit up in surprise and fright, for I do not think he was expecting what was now standing before him. "I am giving you one chance to save the lives of you and your men," Syry stated.

"And how do we do that?" asked the commander.

"Simple, leave!" replied Syry.

"I cannot do that," stated the commander.

"You cannot think that you can win?" Syry asked.

"No, but I have my orders and will not disobey them," replied the commander.

"What would you say to single combat?"

"What are you offering?" asked the commander.

Syry replied. "Your best fighter against me, and if you win, we will leave you in peace, but if I win, you and your men will be free to leave here with your lives intact."

It was surprising to hear these words leave Syry's lips, considering the first battle and her orders then, but I also knew that she would never allow these men to walk away alive.

"Your terms are acceptable; let me fetch my man," replied the commander as Syry gestured towards the mine, signaling him to leave.

It did not take the mine commander long to return with his man. As the commander and his man exited the gate of the mining camp, Syry and Lyra dismounted and walked forward. They stopped a few steps from the rest of us; Lyra helped Syry unbuckle her sword belt as Syry donned her helmet. Syry then took her sword from Lyra and stepped forward as Lyra stepped back. The man with the commander must have stood nearly seven feet tall, which practically dwarfed Syry, but no matter, Syry did not back down as the man stepped forward, hefting his battle ax. Syry let the man make the first move in the dance of death, and while Syry could quickly maneuver herself around this man, she did not; instead, she parried most of his blows, which tired him out. Finally, with an angered rush and strike, the man made a fatal mistake as he struck down with his battle-ax, embedding it in the ground, leaving room for Syry to strike down hard on the man's neck, cleaving his head and spraying blood all around with most of it on Syry.

"The camp is yours, Queen Syry; allow me and men to gather our belongings to leave," stated the commander.

Syry was not even breathing hard after the fight, but as she replied, she kept her back to the commander. "Commander, you and your men can get their stuff, but you will assemble in a line without any weapons, and when I am ready, I will release you."

The commander nodded and visibly shook as he turned around and walked away. By the time the gates of the mining camp reopened, the majority of the army was now at our backs. However, the commander was true to Syry's word in coming out in a line and unarmed, and when they formed up in front of the gates, Syry ordered them to be seized and the slaves freed. As the former guards were being bound, the cheering from the slaves and their families was almost deafening, and they quickly swarmed around Syry, lifting her. After some time, they finally put Syry down and started to attack their former captures, but Syry ordered them off, for which the commander was very thankful.

"Do not thank me yet, commander. Takari, bring your man forward," Syry ordered.

In the two days since leaving Totia, Syry had learned the names of her new commanders. Takari obeyed as she shoved the man forward and stopped him short of Syry. Syry pulled her dagger and gutted the man. "On his knees!"

Syry ordered Takari to force the balling man down onto his knees, and then Syry drew her sword and cleaved his head free.

"You gave me your word that we would be free!" shouted the former commander.

Syry did not reply but instead repeated the gutting and the cleaving of heads for the remaining twenty-nine guards. By the time she had finished with the thirty guards, the commander was balling like a baby and pleading for his life. Syry walked over to him and sharply grabbed his hair, leering closely.

"I never gave my word. Besides, you and your men have done far worse to my people," Syry stated as she cut his pants free; the man soiled himself, but Syry could not care less as she severed the man's manhood and shoved it in his mouth just before she gutted him and cleaved his head.

After the deed was done, Syry was covered in the blood of the former guards and had ordered that each head be erected on a pike while the bodies were piled and burned. After all of this, Syry walked away to a nearby stream and began to strip her armor so that she could cleanse herself. Lyra followed after her, along with Takari and Maith, who also ordered for Syry's tent to be erected nearby, giving her peace and privacy. Meanwhile, the rest of us tended to the slaves and took stock of the mine and its supplies. It was not until late evening that Syry showed herself since the be-headings, and despite the gruesome task she had performed, she had a light of ease about her and a smile on her face as she emerged from her tent. At this, we were still tending to the many former slaves. Many of them asked about her because they wanted to know more about her, and most tried to answer their questions. During most of it, I kept watch near her tent; in part, I wanted to go to her, to talk and comfort her if needed, but I knew Lyra was better suited for that. At first, I did not see her come from her tent until she walked towards me as I tended to my weapons and armor.

"Father, how are things here?" Syry asked.

I replied and asked. "Many are still trying to tend to the needs of the former slaves. How are you feeling?"

"Part of me regrets my decision to execute those guards," Syry replied.

"Because they were defenseless?"

"Yeah," Syry replied as I pulled her into my arms and onto my lap, holding her like a child.

"Syry, listen to me. Those men were neither defenseless nor innocent. They chose to live their lives and got what they deserved. Was it a wise choice to do the job yourself? I cannot answer this, but I will say this: you are taking back the lands, the people who deserve their freedom, and you are taking vengeance on the people who destroyed your home and your family," I stated while still holding her.

"Thank you, Father," Syry replied.

"You are welcome. Come, let us find you food."

Both Syry and I left my gear where I was sitting and wondered among the various groups, with many of them preparing their meals, which all of them offered her, and she sampled almost every meal being cooked. As we neared the gate leading to the former slave quarters, the children of the former slaves were dancing, playing, cheering, and running about. It comforted Syry, knowing she was responsible for this and that they would never have to live under these conditions again.

Just as we crossed over the threshold of the gate, we were greeted by an elder. "Queen Syry, please join us; come sit at our fire, hear the laughter of our children, whose lives you saved," before Syry could object or say anything, half a dozen children pulled her to the fire where several elves tended to a large cauldron and several roasting rabbits. "Leave her be, children. Sorry about that, Queen Syry."

"Please call me Syry, and it is quite alright. It is good for the soul to hear and be around children who do not have care in this world. I am sorry I did not catch your name."

"Que… Sorry, Syry. My name is Elasha. I am the oldest among us, so many consider me the Elder," stated Elasha.

"Thank you, Elasha. I cannot imagine what your people here have gone through" Syry replied.

"Syry, that does not matter anymore, for we are no longer the slaves of Koyla and his men, and you dealt with them the only clean way of doing so. Death," Elasha remarked.

"There you are, Puisín," Lyra stated, causing Syry to turn towards the gate.

"Lyra," Syry extended her arm, beckoning her to join her, and she gave Syry a kiss when she sat behind her as Syry moved from the stump to the ground, which allowed herself to lie back into Lyra's lap and arms. Syry could tell that Elasha was disturbed by her affection for Lyra. "Elasha, this is Lyra, my mate."

"Welcome, Lyra. This is a surprising joining. Would either of you care for anything to eat or drink?" asked Elasha.

"No, thank you, Elasha," replied Syry and Lyra.

As Syry and Lyra relaxed, the children began to dance and sing. Shortly after the children started to sing and dance, Syry began to hum almost in perfect tune to the song, and as she did this, a child no more than four years old climbed into Syry's lap and just lay there for the remainder of the evening. It took Elasha some time to figure out that the child was sitting in Syry's lap and rushed over.

"Leave the Queen alone. Come away from her," commanded Elasha as she tried to convince the child to leave Syry's lap.

"It is alright, Elasha. She is not harming anything," Syry stated as she held off Elasha from bending down to pick the child up. Elasha then turned and went back to taking care of the other children. Meanwhile, I kept to the background, out of sight from almost everyone. I had my reasons for keeping away from the enjoyment that surrounded Syry and Lyra.

"You should join them, you old fuddy-duddy," stated a voice.

I turned at the touch upon my shoulder and the voice speaking out of the darkness. Replying. "Who are you calling old? You are not a hatchling yourself, Sewa."

"I know Ma'yta would want you to enjoy Syry's happiness," Sewa retorted.

"Sewa, I made a promise years ago never to don my armor nor to pick up my sword, and I have broken that promise...." I stated as Sewa interrupted me.

"It needed to be broken, for Syry needed your love and, more importantly, your protection. So go be part of her life," Sewa stated as she tried pushing me towards the group and Syry, but I held firm.

"No, I will spoil the moment for her, and I do not want that," I replied as I turned away from watching Syry and tried returning to my former spot, but Sewa stopped me.

"Why will not you go and be part of her night?" asked Sewa.

I replied. "She needs to be around as much happiness as possible, and my current mood would affect that." But unfortunately, Sewa still was not allowing me to leave, so I tried again to move past her.

"What else is bugging you, old man?" asked Sewa.

"I want to remember her like this, happy and not what I fear will come," I stated as I looked back at Syry and finally pushed past Sewa, leaving her guessing what I meant and feared.

Chapter 14

Marching to War

After leaving Syry alone for the remainder of the evening, I returned to my spot and tried to sleep, but that proved fruitless. Come morning, the camp was waking up, and it did not take long for the leaders of the rebel groups and several members of the former slaves to talk around a makeshift table, discussing the next step. Likewise, it did not take long for Syry and Lyra to join them, both in full armor and for my people to assemble with them.

"Are you discussing what to do next without me?" Syry asked as she stood at the edge of the group.

"I am sorry, my Queen, we did not want to disturb you yet," stated Laiex.

"Well, all someone had to do was to check to see if I was awake. Let's put that behind us and focus on what is before us," replied Syry as she approached the table. There was silent approval of nodding heads. "So, what were we discussing?" she asked.

"My Queen, we were discussing what we should do next," stated Laiex

"Well, I need to rejoin Elder Lomman, the rest of the elders, and the rest of my army at Lo'karan. So now, those who came with me and I will travel to Lo'karan. Laiex, I want you to stay with these people and your soldiers as they travel behind us...." Syry raised her hand to keep Laiex from objecting as he wanted to. "…I want fifty riders to join me. Now, you may speak Laiex," Syry commanded.

"My Queen, Lo'karan will take several days to reach, especially with everyone here present, and what of the children we rescued from this pit," Laiex stated as he gestured around him at his last remark.

"Syry, I can answer that."

"Hycis, correct?" Syry asked, and he nodded in return.

Hycis replied. "Let a small group of us take the children and those too old or frail to fight back to Totia, where we can at least take better care of them."

"Elasha, I can tell you do not agree with this," Syry stated.

"No, I do not, Syry. My people, including the children, are not about to sit out after what we have been through, and those who might be too old to fight will not hear of it, as they have even more of a reason than most present to fight," stated Elasha.

Syry commanded rather than stated. "Then the matter is settled; everyone will come. I will not argue about my decision; I want them obeyed. Now, Cohnal, choose which warriors you want to join you as you go with me."

I could tell that the order took aback Cohnal.

"Syry, I think Takari would be better for your orders," I stated as I leaned toward her from behind.

"Why, father?" Syry asked.

"Takari and the majority of her riders are skilled horse archers. Meaning, they move fast, which will aid us in making it to Lo'karan as quickly as possible," I replied.

"Thank you, father," Syry replied and asked. "Takari, you and your soldiers are skilled archers on horseback, correct?"

"Correct, my Queen. We are; we can ride fast and hit everything we aim at," Takari replied.

"Very good. Cohnal, disregard my order. Takari, see to my request in selecting your soldiers," Syry ordered.

"Yes, my Queen, I will select my best," replied Takari as she moved off and started selecting her soldiers.

"My Queen, thank you for making the change, but I would still like to come."

"Why, Cohnal?" Syry asked.

"Takari is my daughter, and I would like the chance to stay close, for we have never really been apart for more than a day," replied Cohnal.

"Granted," Syry replied and asked. "Is there anything further that needs to be discussed?"

"No, my Queen." Laiex stated as everyone looked at Syry.

"Laiex, you have your orders, and I will see all of you in time when we meet at Lo'karan," Syry stated and then turned about, leaving the rest to their tasks or to discuss further how they would move out while Takari and my people gathered our belongings and prepared to ride out with Syry for Lo'karan.

It took us several days of travel from that now deserted iron mine to the city fortress of Lo'karan. When we had arrived, we found Syry's banner, a white raven upon a purple field—flying from the ramparts and the path lined with the severed heads of the soldiers and the remains of their bodies still smoldering upon their pyres. One of my people, Da'kaalth, was standing watch at the gate and gave a shout when he saw us approaching. At the time of arrival, I was riding in the lead with Syry and Lyra right behind, with the rest of my people riding up alongside and behind them. As we reined up, the ramparts began to bustle with troops cheering for Syry.

"Da'kaalth, I see that Lo'karan was successfully taken," stated Syry as she came alongside me.

"It was successful," stated Da'kaalth.

"Any losses on our part?" Syry asked.

He replied. "Only a few."

"How few Da'kaalth?"

"Less than a dozen, Syry. They gave up pretty quick."

"Any innocents harmed?"

"Only two or three."

"Very good. Da'kaalth, will you help Takari find accommodations for these people?" Syry asked as she gestured behind her.

I was surprised that Da'kaalth did not object to the request. After that brief exchange, Syry urged her horse forward and made her way to the central keep of the city, where we found the elders and the rest of my people waiting for her arrival.

After our arrival and for the next four or five days, Syry and all the various leaders discussed the next steps in the war and what to do with Lo'karan. In the end, Syry was adamant about waging total war on Koyla and those who serve him. So in the morning that her forces marched from Lo'karan, she ordered that the city be burned to the ground, but she did give the people of Lo'karan a chance to leave before the burning.

For the next nine months, we fought seven battles without losing a single one, and while we did suffer losses, our numbers continued to grow; before long, the numbers swelled above five thousand, with about half of them on horseback. Most of the battles never earned a name, but most of them did have a place name or were near a place. Surprisingly, I can recall the approximate date on which they occurred: Oak Creek and Elks Groove on the 6th and 20th of Biotáille Abhaile (November) 1246, Willow Hill on the 7th of Taibhsí Sinsear (December) 1246, Brea Plains the 13th of Íogair (March) 1247, Tummel River and Perth the 1st and 15th of Bláth Beacha (May) 1247, and Leven 6th of Sciatháin Féileacán (June) 1247. The last battle of the Vengeance War changed the lives of many and is not mentioned here, but it will be in time.

Chapter 15

Goddess, a Debt Repaid

After the battle at Leven on the 6th of Sciatháin Féileacán (June) 1247, we made our way to the small town of Alloa, and on the 18th, we arrived, finding the place deserted, which was not all that surprising considering we were only a few days march from Sitthi. Over the next day, we continued to fortify the town and set up defenses. Despite the typical cloudy, drizzly weather, spirits were high, and many were looking forward to the end of the war, and the destruction of the Sitthi Kingdom, and the end of Koyla. This was true most of all for Syry, who had grown quite temperamental over the last few days.

However, on the morning of the 20th, her temperament was about to be unleashed. That morning, Koyla had sneaked up on the camp, and just as the sun was breaching the eastern sea, he launched his attack. It caught us off guard as most were still asleep, but the leaders and the officers quickly made sense of what was happening and formed up and started to fight back. Sadly, most wore no armor because of the time of day, which shortened their lives. Myself, Kul'seair, Te'jo, Cedah, and Ya'tui rallied to Syry, who was quickly leaving her tent wearing only half her armor, and Lyra scrambling after her. Syry did not wait for anyone as she charged head-on into Koyla's ranks, and even being alone at first, she was like a scythe among barley; nothing could withstand her. Finally, we caught up to her and helped clear a path, encouraging her people to follow and fight even harder.

Like the tyrant that Koyla was, he was not leading his men into battle but instead was sitting high on his horse, ordering from the back. After we had regrouped, Syry quickly located Koyla before anyone could say or do anything to prevent her from disappearing like smoke and heading for Koyla. When she reappeared, she hit Koyla's horse like a stone, causing it to throw him from the saddle. Despite this, he quickly found his footing and braced for Syry's attack. For the next several moments, we fought our way to her while she battled Koyla; I do not know who wanted to get to her faster, Lyra or myself.

That battle meant everything for both of them; for Syry, it meant revenge for her parent's death, and for Koyla, it meant the end of both a dynasty and a rebellion. While I never questioned Syry's ability to fight, I knew this would be her most brutal fight as Koyla was a veteran fighter, and he knew how to fight, but Syry was younger and faster. As they battled, the battle around them continued, and thankfully, no one moved in to help Koyla win, for if they did, we would have stopped them. Sadly, I saw Syry's temper rise the longer the fight continued, making her careless in attacks and defenses. A fortunate mistake of Koyla's allowed Syry to strike hard down on his back, but his cuirass took the brunt of the hit, and even though he was down on one knee, he was successfully keeping Syry at bay, which just angered her even more.

After several grueling moments of back-and-forth fighting for Syry and Koyla, Koyla was beginning to tire, which left himself open to attack. Syry used her ability to disappear to make her final move. Unfortunately, Koyla saw it coming and was ready. When Syry reappeared and struck home her final blow, Koyla was ready, and at the moment before her sword bit into the back of his neck, he punched his sword back, and it hit home, piercing her just below her heart. But her aim never missed, and her sword cleaved into Koyla's neck, ending his life. Syry stumbled away as both Lyra and I ran to her; I caught her just before she fell. As I caught her, I slammed to my knees and pulled her into my arms. Lyra grabbed onto both of us as Syry looked up, watching Morna circling overhead.

Syry cradled my face for a moment before she spoke. "I am sorry, Father, I will not be returning home with you. My debt is repaid," as Syry spoke, Lyra looked up and saw that Morna was no longer alone. "I am sorry, my love…."

"Syry, Puisín! No," Lyra shouted and grabbed onto Syry as Syry's hand fell from my face, and her eyes closed.

I wrapped my arms around them both, pulling them even closer. I do not know how long the silence had lasted, but when I finally looked about the whole field, all of my people stood nearby except for Kul'seair, Syry's grandfather, who kneeled just behind me. Even with my watered eyes, I could see the sadness that had descended upon everyone. But what happened next has stayed with me for several hundred years. As I continued to hold Lyra and Syry, I saw, as some would say, a ghost; I saw Ella, Syry's mother, appear, followed by Danu; there were a few others I recognized but could not recall names. As I looked upon these ghostly figures, I felt a touch like a feather gently grazing my cheek, and for that moment of contact, I looked down at Syry; when I looked back up, I saw Syry standing with her parents wearing not her regular pants and shirt but instead the red and black wedding gown she had worn when she and Lyra formalized their bonding.

"Lyra, look," I urged.

"Wha… what?" Lyra asked as she looked at me. I gently turned her head towards Syry's ghostly form. "Puisín?" she asked.

Syry replied. "Hush, love. I know you may not understand this, but a debt must be repaid, and it has. In time, my love, your loss will heal. Father, thank you for everything."

I could not respond; my grief continued as I held onto Syry. The next moment, Syry's ghost looked around the battlefield and lifted her hands like a summoning one to rise. As she did this, every spirit of elven, dwarven, and some human fallen warriors rose from their fallen spots and joined her.

When this happened, many humans dropped to their knees, almost in fear of what they were seeing, and many of them and some of the elves said, *Goddess.* In my people's language, the closest thing that relates is spirit-fairy. After that moment, Syry and the spirits of her fallen soldiers disappeared like smoke in the wind. Slowly, everyone started clearing the field of the dead, and in doing so, they all gave Lyra and myself a wide berth. A few days after that sad day, we finally burned Syry's body and gathered the ashes into the same chest that held the Royal Crown of Totia.

The remaining humans loyal to Koyal surrendered without cause and kept to their word that they would not cause any problems. A few days later, on the 28th of

Sciatháin Féileacán (June) 1247, Laiex and a few others marched and took control of the city Sitthi. This day marked the end of the Vengeance War and the end of a dynasty.

Chapter 16

A Shadows Honor

It has been almost three hundred years since Syry's death, and during this time, it has amazed me that the term Goddess has spread among the elves, and many refer to her by that name when they ask for her guidance or strength. I do not know whether this is because they fear her spoken name or do not know her name. However, it brings me comfort to know that her spirit lives on. After the battle at Alloa had ended and the dead were tended to, Kul'seair wreaked absolute havoc on Koyla's body as he tore it apart and smashed it like pudding. Nothing was left except mush, and no one even dared to claim the remains to burn.

Three days after the battle had ended, we finally burned Syry's remains on the most enormous pyre I had ever seen; Kul'seair had seen to this. Lyra was the one who lit the pyre, and it took two full days for it to burn completely. During those two days, Lyra, Kul'seair, Meesha'ka, and I never left the pyre as it burned. During the early hours of the second day, Morna landed in the middle of the pyre and stayed there, thus ending her life and binding her spirit with Syry's. After the fire burned down and the coals cooled to ash, we collected Syry's ashes and placed them within the chest that held Totia's crown. After all of this, the four of us debated what to do next, and it was agreed that we would go north to Szczyt Śnieżnej Wiśni or Ben Macdui in the common tongue.

Once we reached Szczyt Śnieżnej Wiśni, we buried the chest at the base of the Stoneheart Tree on the southern slope and settled near a small elven village controlled by Lyra's clan. Sadly, just thirty years after we settled here, Kul'seair passed away at the age of 2,275, but within those thirty years, Lyra bore a daughter that she said was from Syry. She said Syry came to her in a dream and told her she would bear the fruit of their union within a moon or two. During those last years, Kul'seair always smiled as he saw Lyra blossom and the little girl that followed; to say that, the little girl always has us wrapped around her little fingers.

Looking back at these pages and the years that have passed, I will never be able to tell all of Syry, for much of it is still too personal, and some I have forgotten. However, over the years that Kul'seair still had left, we often heard tales of Syry, of how a young elven woman stood up and destroyed a human kingdom; many of the stories were not always accurate, but they did not matter as they kept her spirit alive. After the Vengeance War ended and the Sitthi kingdom was destroyed, the remaining elven people went their way, and none returned to Totia. From what I have been told, the fallen city had finally collapsed, and the stains finally washed away, leaving the city to turn to dust and be reclaimed by the land.

Excuse me, Syry and Lyra's daughter interrupted me, asking me to help her with her bow and arrow. This is the last I will write; for now, I need to rest, but more importantly, it is time for Syry to sleep, and I know her spirit will live on.

Death and Honor,
A'kull of Clan Ta'lo'c
> *Shadows Ghost in Blood and Honor.*

Appendix A: General Knowledge

Aeshies

Aeshies or Sapphire Lily, as some would call it. The Aeshies have an almost sickly sweet smell of a rose and a lily. It has the shape of a five-pointed star with each of its petals a deep sapphire blue color with a blood red stripe down the middle with white stripes residing along each side of the blood red stripe within the sapphire blue colored petals. The petals are harmless; however, down at the root bulb of the flower, down in its leathery bulb is where you find Blood-salts, already in crystal form. The Blood-salts smell of blood, unlike the flower from which it comes, and are quite deadly.

Ardara

It is an Elven village located near the base of Snow Lynx Mountain and just on the edge of Lough Claire—map location G-2.

Bay of Firth of Forth

Firth of Forth lies on the eastern shore of Ellrifold, and the River Annan flows from the bay—map location E-6.

Ben Macdui - Buaic Silíní Sneachta

It is one of the highest peaks in Ellrifold and is located in the northeast part of Ellrifold and lies west of Loch Ness. Its common tongue name is Ben Macdui. Its name in the

Elvish tongue is Buaic Silíní Sneachta. Its name in the forgotten tongue is Szczyt Śnieżnej Wiśni. Both of the elvish and forgotten tongue names translate to Snow Cherry Peak—map location: C-6.

Blood-salts

Blood-salts come from a rare flower called Aeshies or Sapphire Lily, as some would call it. The Aeshies have an almost sickly sweet smell of a rose and a lily. It has the shape of a five-pointed star with each of its petals a deep sapphire blue color with a blood red stripe down the middle with white stripes residing along each side of the blood red stripe within the sapphire blue colored petals. The petals are harmless; however, down at the root bulb of the flower, down in its leathery bulb, is where you find blood-salts, already in crystal form. The Blood-salts smell like blood, unlike the flower they come from, and they are quite deadly.

Calendars of Ellrifold

The Uthuk-Nari founded the calendar system 3,500 years before the Elves, Dwarves, and Humans adopted and established their own calendar systems, which are based on the Uthuk-Nari System. An example of a year date between the Uthuk-Nari and any of the others: *[Uthuk-Nari]* 18th of Zbezcześcić (September) 4746, *[Elvish]* 18th of Truaill an Tsaoil (September) 1246.

Uthuk-Nari Calendar

Month-days - meaning - Uthuk-Nari name:
January 1-31 - fairy - Wróżka
February 1-28 - ghost - Duch
March 1-31 - delicate - Delikatny
April 1-30 - blossoming - Kwitnące
May 1-31 - bee - Pszczoła
June 1-30 - butterfly - Motyl
July 1-31 - tranquil - Cichy
August 1-31 - fury - Furia
September 1-30 - defile - Zbezcześcić
October 1-31- cursed - Przeklęty
November 1-30 - soul - Dusza
December 1-31 - fairy of death - Wróżka Śmierci

Dwarvish Calendar

Month-days - meaning - Dwarvish name:
January 1-31 - fires ghost - Feuert Geist
February 1-28 - snows fury - Schnees Wut
March 1-31 - deaths stone - Todesstein
April 1-30 - hunters blood - Jäger Blut
May 1-31 - hunters stone - Jäger Stein
June 1-30 - deaths wrath - Zorn des Todes
July 1-31 - fires embrace - Feuer Umarmen
August 1-31 - silver fires - Silberne Feuer
September 1-30 - stone heart - Steinherz
October 1-31- snows ghost - Schneegeist
November 1-30 - snows drink - Schnee trinken
December 1-31 - hearths warmth - Feuerstellen Wärme

Elvish Calendar

Month-days - meaning - Elvish name:
January 1-31 - fairy snow- Sneachta Sióg
February 1-28 - ghost - Púca
March 1-31 - delicate - Íogair
April 1-30 - blossom - Bhláth
May 1-31 - bee flower- Bláth Beacha
June 1-30 - butterfly wings - Sciatháin Féileacán
July 1-31 - haven - Caladh
August 1-31 - fury - Feall
September 1-30 - life's defile - Truaill an Tsaoil
October 1-31- cursed lives - Saolta Mallaithe
November 1-30 - spirits home - Biotáille Abhaile
December 1-31 - ancestors ghosts - Taibhsí Sinsear

Human Calendar

Month-days:
January 1-31
February 1-28
March 1-31
April 1-30
May 1-31
June 1-30
July 1-31
August 1-31
September 1-30
October 1-31
November 1-30
December 1-31

Currency of Ellrifold

The most common currency used is the Dwarven, and if not used, most kingdoms base their currency on that of the Dwarves. The Dwarves are the only ones who have established a banking system spread throughout Ellrifold. Some humans have established their own banks but only spread inside their home city or territory. Traditionally, Elves do not use coinage, as they rely on trade between themselves, but will use coinage when commercing with Humans, Dwarves, and Orcs. Orcs do not have their own currency, so they often rely on Dwarven currency.

Dwarven Banking: (most common currency)
 Pound (gold) = 10 shillings or 100 pennies
 Shilling (silver) = 10 pennies
 Penny (copper)
 Pinig (iron) = 1 pound + 5 shilling

Brejoc Currency: This is double the Dwarven coinage, and it is not widely used and eventually becomes obsolete.
 Stosakel: (gold) = 2 pounds or 20 shillings or 200 pennies
 Styqgeni: (silver) = 2 shillings or 20 pennies
 Okni: (copper) = 2 pennies

Dunnagall

It is located on the far western shore of Ellrifold, on the west side of the great Elven and Dwarven city of Valhalla—map location: G-2.

Ellrifold

This means the elder world; it is the home to Elves, Dwarves, Orcs, Humans, and various other creatures. It stretches over 2500 miles from its farthest Northern to Southern points and more than 2000 miles from East to West.

Kent

It is a human-ruled city that lies South of the River Trent and west of the Dwarven Mountains, Berg Schmieden(Forge Mountain), and Silberner Feuerberg (Silver Fire Mountain)—map location: G-7.

Ket

Ket is a village on Ka'leen Bay. It is home to mainly Elves, but a few Humans and Dwarves also live there—map location: E-4.

Lo'karan, Siege

A fortified city under Koyla's control. Syry's army sacked it under the general command of Elven Elder Lomman in September 1246. The only people surviving the siege were the women, the children, and any elder beyond fighting age—map location: F-5.

Mage Lites

A quartz crystal made by mages to give off light without producing a flame. Instead, they cast a yellow-white light to an almost blinding white when rubbed between someone's hands.

Puisín

Puisín *(pu-sheen)* means kitten in the Elvish tongue. A term of affection that Lyra used for Syry.

Races of Ellrifold
Druids

The Druids are built like Humans and have a similar lifespan. They primarily tend to various Stoneheart Trees and the grooves that surround them. They are also called upon to help negotiate terms between rival sides. Their most unique attribute is their almost glowing orange eyes.

Dwarves

Dwarves are built of heavy stock and stand under five feet on average. They are some of the best artisans and craftsmen around Ellrifold. They often prefer to keep their mountains and mines. They also breed the Dwarven Mastiff, a war hound that stands just under three feet at their shoulders. They also prefer heavy steel plate armor over any other kind. They are a patriarchal people. They live an average of 400-600 years.

Elves

Elves are generally lean and fit. They stand, on average, six feet tall but will often reach seven feet tall. Their pointed ears are their most prominent feature. They are some of the fastest runners and are light on their feet. They prefer light to medium-weight armor consisting of steel plate, mail, and leather. Most live in clan groups away from human cities. They are a matriarchal people. They live an average of 400-1000 years.

Humans

Humans stand an average of six feet. They are built like a cross between Elves' slender nature and the robustness of Orcs' but lack the strength of Orcs. Humans often live in cities and villages. They frequently view other races as below them, which has led to many wars between them and the different races. They are a patriarchal people. They live an average of 100 years.

Orcs

Orcs often stand between seven and nine feet tall. While they are not the fastest, they are almost unmatched in strength. Many clans roam about, but some have settled within what they call Strongholds. They are a patriarchal people. They live an average of 400-600 years.

Uthuk-Nari

The Uthuk-Nari are a long-forgotten race, and very little is known about them. However, many stand more than seven feet tall, with many standing closer to ten feet tall. They have an incredibly long life span, longer than Elves. They are patriarchal, but it is not uncommon for the children to take after their mother's family name if their mother was an Elf.

Rite of Ancestors Blood - Obrzęd Krwi Przodków

The Rite of Ancestors Blood or, in the forgotten tongue, Obrzęd Krwi Przodków, is about trying to summon the spirits of one's ancestors to guide them to another of blood or ancestor. In order for the rite to work correctly, both a potion and an incantation must be used before the Stoneheart Tree.

The potion contents:
Ashes of Aeshies flower (blood-salt flower), a shaving sliver or two from a Stoneheart Tree, spirits, and a small amount of the takers' blood.

The Uthuk-Nari incantation:
"Blood of my blood, come to me, ancestors of my blood aid me, guide me to my blood. Ancestors hear my call, blood of my blood hear me, blood by blood, life, and death guide me to those that are lost."

Silken Seam

A small tailor shop in the walled city of Kent, founded by the Elves Tina and Hal. The shop also consisted of a lower level hidden beneath the shop that they used to help other Elves escape the northern realms.

Sitthi Kingdom

The Sitthi Kingdom was founded by Koyla's father, Vortigern, who built the castle and town of Sitthi on the ocean bay of Firth of Forth, the kingdom's seat of power. Its borders spread 250 miles north and south of its seat of power and to the western shore of Ellrifold. The kingdom lasted from the year 1198 to the year 1247 of the Human calendar.

Sitthi Town & Castle

The town and castle of Sitthi were established by Vortigern, Koyla's father, in 1198 of the Human calendar. The town and castle were the seats of power for the Sitthi Kingdom. After the Vengeance War ended in 1247 of the Human calendar, the city and castle were renamed Edinburgh— map location: E-6.

Stonefeather Cat (Hakari)

The Stonefeather Cat or Hakari in the Elvish tongue measures about 8 feet in length from head to tail, stands about 28 inches tall, and can weigh up to 150 lbs. In general, males and females are often the same size. Their fur resembles feathers, and their coats vary in color from all gray and black to a mix of gray, black, and reddish brown. An interesting note about their feathered fur is that it can turn into a stone-like hardness, offering protection, which is often impenetrable; despite this stone-like hardness, their fur is quite soft. Unfortunately, because of this ability, they have been hunted to the brink of extinction for their fur, which retains this impenetrable quality after being skinned. Their eyes are either yellow or green in color.

Stoneheart Tree

Stoneheart Trees gets its name for two reasons. The first is that its limbs and trunk are like stone, meaning nothing can cut them. The second reason is that its leaves are shaped like a heart. Its leaves are blood red in color. Its bark is pale white, almost bone-white in color. It smells of cinnamon, lilies, roses, and a sweetness like honey. They are sacred to many of the cultures of Ellrifold and, therefore, are highly respected and often play a significant role in the lives of the cultures of Ellrifold. Oftentimes, ceremonies like marriages, burial rites, coming of age, name taking, are often done in front of them. Because of their significance, they are also seen as the connection between the living and their ancestors. In general, many of the Stoneheart Trees are often found within Druid's grooves, and the Druids are often seen as priests, even though there is no set religion in Ellrifold.

Syry's Banner

Syry's banner is a white raven flying upon a purple field.

Ta'neek

An Elven village that lies about 250 miles West of Kent. The town makes its living raising sheep for wool and meat and trading various Elven goods from nearby clans—map Location: H-6.

Totia

The Elven city of Totia was the seat of power for the Totia Kingdom and was ruled by an Elven King and Queen. The city lies on the western shore of Ellrifold and north of Ayr Mountain. The city fell in 1215 to Koyla's forces and was never rebuilt after the completion of the Vengeance War when it ended in 1250—map location: E-5.

Totia, Crown of

The crown is made of Trinthi'ium and gold twisted together with six blood-diamonds studded around it. A Uthuk-Nari smith made it for the royal family.

Totia Kingdom

The Totia Kingdom was an Elven kingdom ruled from the city of Totia on Ellrifold's western shore. It was founded around 1065 and lasted until 1215 when it fell to Koyla. King Danu of Clan Ayr and Queen Ella of Clan Ailsa were the last kings and queens to rule the kingdom until their daughter Syry was crowned in 1246 of the Elven calendar.

Trinthi'ium

A metal that is lighter than steel or iron and so much stronger. It is said that it is unbreakable. The metal smiths of the Elves and the Dwarves are most often considered masters of crafting trinthi'ium, but a few Human smiths have also learned how to. It can also be forged mixed with steel, resulting in an alloy lighter than a steel sword but far stronger than an all-steel sword. This mix is often referred to as Valhalla-forged, as the mountain of Valhalla is where most of this alloy mix initially came from. Its true origin is unknown to later scholars and forge masters of Ellrifold, but it is thought to have been created by Uthuk-Nari, a long-forgotten and extinct race.

Twins: The

The Twins are Snow Raven Mountain in the north and Snow Lynx Mountain in the south—map location G-1/2. The Twins are a pair of mountains on the far western shore of Ellrifold, located west of Lough Claire and west-southwest of Drumard Bay. Its Elvish name is Na Cúpla, or the forgotten tongue Bliźniacy. They are also the tallest mountains in Ellrifold, and because of their height, their peaks are often covered in snow year-round.

Snow Lynx Mountain

Its name in the Elvish tongue is Sliabh Púca, or in the forgotten tongue, is Góra Ryś Śnieżny. Unlike its northern sister, Snow Raven Mountain, its interior was never carved out into living spaces; instead, its lower slopes were home to a few remote family homes of Elves and Dwarves.

Snow Raven Mountain

Its name in the Elvish tongue is Sliabh Préachán Sneachta, or in the forgotten tongue, Śnieżna Góra Kruka. The mountain was often considered to be the home of the Uthuk-Nari, but unfortunately, after a time, it was abandoned and considered haunted. Therefore, no one would ever trespass on those long-forgotten halls.

Valhalla

Valhalla is the second tallest mountain in Ellrifold, and it was once home to the great Elven and Dwarven city, also known by the same as the mountain itself. It is located in the far western region of Ellrifold—map location: G-3. It is east of Drumard Bay and the Dwarven trade port

Dunnagall. It is just northeast of Lough Claire. It was once home to the great Elven and Dwarven smiths, acclaimed for making Valhalla-forged steel alloys. Unfortunately, this great city was eventually abandoned, but when or why this great city was abandoned is unknown. Plus, many believe the ruins to be cursed.

Vengeance War

The Vengeance War was about Syry's vengeance for her parent's death and the destruction of her family's kingdom. Syry and her allies land north of the Elven village of Ta'neek on the 20th of Feall (August) 1246. The war ended on the 28th of Sciatháin Féileacán (June) 1247, with the surrender of the city Sitthi. Syry and her allies never lost a battle throughout the war, but unfortunately, in the end, the war claimed Syry's life.

Battles:

1 of 11 Battle against General Dannern on the 18th of Truaill an Tsaoil (September) 1246. Map location: F-5.

2 of 11 Battle and siege of Lo'karan in the month of Truaill an Tsaoil (September) 1246. Map location: F-5.

3 of 11 Oak Creek on the 6th of Biotáille Abhaile (November) 1246. Map location: E-5.

4 of 1 Elks Groove on the 20th of Biotáille Abhaile (November) 1246. Map location: D-5.

5 of 11 Willow Hill on the 7th of Taibhsí Sinsear (December) 1246. Map location: D-5.

6 of 11 Brea Plains on the 13th of Íogair (March) 1247. Map location: D-5.

7 of 11 Tummel River on the 1st of Bláth Beacha (May) 1247. Map location: D-5.

8 of 11 Perth on the 15th of Bláth Beacha (May) 1247. Map location: D-6.

9 of 11 Leven on the 6th of Sciatháin Féileacán (June) 1247. Map location: E-6.

10 of 11 Alloa on the 20th of Sciatháin Féileacán (June) 1247. Map location: E-5.

11 of 11 Sitthi on the 28th of Sciatháin Féileacán (June) 1247. Map location: E-6.

Appendix B: Characters

Book Abbreviations
TBG - The Birth of a Goddess
AAC - An Ancestors Curse
ADG - A Dragons Gift

A'dqaar

Race: Uthuk-Nari
Sex: Male
Birth-Death: ***
Height: ***
Hair Color: ***
Eye Color: ***
Family Name: ***
Father's Name: ***
Mother's Family Name: ***
Mother's Name: ***
Spouse's Name: ***
Marriage Date: ***
Children: ***
Miscellaneous Information:
His favored weapon is the battle-ax. He was 1 of 21 who joined Syry to fight alongside her and free her family's kingdom.
Books: TBG

A'kull Clan Ta'lo'c

Race: Uthuk-Nari
Sex: Male
Birth-Death: ***
Height: 8ft~
Hair Color: ***
Eye Color: ***
Family Name: Clan Ta'lo'c
Father's Name: ***
Mother's Family Name: ***
Mother's Name: ***
Spouse's Name: Ma'yta
Marriage Date: ***
Children: E'yti
Miscellaneous Information:
The blood groove of his bastard blade is inscribed with-Blood and Death is Life Anew. Is brother to Ha'thap. "Death and Honor" is a common saying between Ha'thap and himself. He was known as the butcher Ka'leen Bay. He has the ability to read another person's mind with nothing but a simple touch. He often wears a necklace with a silver skull of a raven. Rode an all-white female shire leaving Kent and another all-white shire during the Vengeance War. He saved Syry as a baby shortly before her mother passed. He was 1 of 21 who joined Syry to fight alongside her and free her family's kingdom.
Books: TBG

Alok

Race: Elf
Sex: Male

Birth-Death: ***
Height: ***
Hair Color: ***
Eye Color: ***
Father's Family Name: ***
Father's Name: ***
Family Name: ***
Mother's Name: ***
Spouse's Name: ***
Marriage Date: ***
Children: ***
Miscellaneous Information: ***
Books: TBG

Ankou

Race: Uthuk-Nari
Sex: Male
Birth-Death: ***
Height: ***
Hair Color: ***
Eye Color: ***
Family Name: ***
Father's Name: ***
Mother's Family Name: ***
Mother's Name: ***
Spouse's Name: ***
Marriage Date: ***
Children: ***
Miscellaneous Information: ***
Books: TBG

Arawa

Race: Uthuk-Nari
Sex: Female
Birth-Death: ***
Height: ***
Hair Color: ***
Eye Color: ***
Family Name: ***
Father's Name: ***
Mother's Family Name: ***
Mother's Name: ***
Spouse's Name: Ha'thap Clan Ta'lo'c
Marriage Date: ***
Children: ***
Occupation: Shopkeeper
Miscellaneous Information: ***
Books: TBG

Arma

Race: Elf
Sex: Female
Birth-Death: ***
Height: ***
Hair Color: ***
Eye Color: ***
Father's Family Name: ***
Father's Name: ***
Family Name: ***
Mother's Name: ***
Spouse's Name: ***
Marriage Date: ***

Children: ***
Occupation: Innkeeper
Miscellaneous Information:
She is a long-time friend of A'kull's.
Books: TBG

Aurae Clan Ailsa

Race: Elf
Sex: Female
Birth-Death: ***
Height: ***
Hair Color: ***
Eye Color: ***
Father's Family Name: ***
Father's Name: ***
Family Name: Clan Ailsa
Mother's Name: ***
Spouse's Name: Kul'seair
Marriage Date: ***
Children: Meesha'ka; Ella
Miscellaneous Information: ***
Books: TBG

Ba'ytup

Race: Uthuk-Nari***
Sex: Male***
Birth-Death: ***
Height: ***
Hair Color: ***
Eye Color: ***
Family Name: ***

Father's Name: ***
Mother's Family Name: ***
Mother's Name: ***
Spouse's Name: ***
Marriage Date: ***
Children: ***
Miscellaneous Information:
He was 1 of 21 who joined Syry to fight alongside her and free her family's kingdom.
Books: TBG

Canku

Race: Uthuk-Nari
Sex: Male***
Birth-Death: ***
Height: ***
Hair Color: ***
Eye Color: ***
Family Name: ***
Father's Name: ***
Mother's Family Name: ***
Mother's Name: ***
Spouse's Name: ***
Marriage Date: ***
Children: ***
Miscellaneous Information:
He was 1 of 21 who joined Syry to fight alongside her and free her family's kingdom. He was one of four, with the others being Da'kaalth, Za'kah, and Gakoal, who traveled with Syry's army to lay siege to Lo'karan.
Books: TBG

Cedah

Race: Uthuk-Nari
Sex: Female
Birth-Death: ***
Height: ***
Hair Color: ***
Eye Color: ***
Family Name: ***
Father's Name: ***
Mother's Family Name: ***
Mother's Name: ***
Spouse's Name: ***
Marriage Date: ***
Children: ***
Miscellaneous Information:
She was 1 of 21 who joined Syry to fight alongside her and free her family's kingdom.
Books: TBG

Cohnal

Race: Elf
Sex: Male
Birth-Death: ***
Height: ***
Hair Color: ***
Eye Color: ***
Father's Family Name: ***
Father's Name: ***
Family Name: ***
Mother's Name: ***
Spouse's Name: ***

Marriage Date: ***
Children: Takari
Occupation: Rebel commander
Miscellaneous Information: ***
Books: TBG

Conri

Race: Elf
Sex: Male
Birth-Death: ***
Height: ***
Hair Color: ***
Eye Color: ***
Father's Family Name: ***
Father's Name: ***
Family Name: ***
Mother's Name: ***
Spouse's Name: ***
Marriage Date: ***
Children: ***
Occupation: ***
Miscellaneous Information:
His middle and ring fingers are down to stubs on his left
hand. He served King Danu and Queen Ella.
Books: TBG

Dahru

Race: Uthuk-Nari
Sex: Male
Birth-Death: ***
Height: ***

Hair Color: ***
Eye Color: ***
Family Name: ***
Father's Name: ***
Mother's Family Name: ***
Mother's Name: ***
Spouse's Name: ***
Marriage Date: ***
Children: ***
Occupation: ***
Miscellaneous Information:
He was 1 of 21 who joined Syry to fight alongside her and free her family's kingdom.
Books: TBG

Da'kaalth

Race: Uthuk-Nari
Sex: Male
Birth-Death: ***
Height: ***
Hair Color: ***
Eye Color: ***
Family Name: ***
Father's Name: ***
Mother's Family Name: ***
Mother's Name: ***
Spouse's Name: ***
Marriage Date: ***
Children: ***
Occupation: ***
Miscellaneous Information:

He was 1 of 21 who joined Syry to fight alongside her and free her family's kingdom. He was one of four, with the others being Za'kah, Canku, and Gakoal, who traveled with Syry's army to lay siege to Lo'karan.
Books: TBG

Da'kian

Race: Uthuk-Nari
Sex: Male
Birth-Death: ***
Height: ***
Hair Color: ***
Eye Color: ***
Family Name: ***
Father's Name: ***
Mother's Family Name: ***
Mother's Name: ***
Spouse's Name: Gaida
Marriage Date: ***
Children: ***
Occupation: ***
Miscellaneous Information: ***
Books: TBG

Dannern

Race: Human
Sex: Male
Birth-Death: (b.)?-(d.)18th of September 1246
Height: ***
Hair Color: ***
Eye Color: ***

Family Name: ***
Father's Name: ***
Mother's Family Name: ***
Mother's Name: ***
Spouse's Name: ***
Marriage Date: ***
Children: ***
Occupation: General
Miscellaneous Information:
He was loyal to Koyla.
Books: TBG

Danu Clan Ayr

Race: Elf
Sex: Male
Birth-Death: (b.)?-(d.)1215
Height: ***
Hair Color: ***
Eye Color: ***
Father's Family Name: ***
Father's Name: ***
Family Name: Clan Ayr
Mother's Name: ***
Spouse's Name: Ella Clan Aisla
Marriage Date: ***
Children: Syry (1216)
Occupation: King
Miscellaneous Information:
Last King of the Totia Kingdom. He died by execution at
the hands of Koyla.
Books: TBG

Elasha

Race: Elf
Sex: Female
Birth-Death: ***
Height: ***
Hair Color: ***
Eye Color: ***
Father's Family Name: ***
Father's Name: ***
Family Name: ***
Mother's Name: ***
Spouse's Name: ***
Marriage Date: ***
Children: ***
Occupation: Elder
Miscellaneous Information:
She was a prisoner at the mining camp north of Totia.
Books: TBG

Ella Clan Ailsa

Race: Elf/Uthuk-Nari
Sex: Female
Birth-Death: (b.)?-(d.)1216
Height: ***
Hair Color: ***
Eye Color: ***
Father's Family Name: ***
Father's Name: Kul'seair
Family Name: Clan Ailsa
Mother's Name: Aurae
Spouse's Name: Danu Clan Ayr

Marriage Date: ***
Children: Syry (1216)
Occupation: Queen
Miscellaneous Information:
She has a heron tattoo on the left side of her neck, just below the jaw. She was injured during her and Syry's escape from Sittthi.
Books: TBG

E'yti Clan Ta'lo'c

Race: Uthuk-Nari
Sex: Female
Birth-Death: ***
Height: ***
Hair Color: ***
Eye Color: ***
Family Name: Clan Ta'lo'c
Father's Name: A'kull
Mother's Family Name: ***
Mother's Name: Ma'yta
Spouse's Name: ***
Marriage Date: ***
Children: ***
Occupation: ***
Miscellaneous Information: ***
Books: TBG

Gaeleath

Race: Elf
Sex: Male
Birth-Death: ***

Height: ~7ft
Hair Color: Brown, cut short
Eye Color: ***
Father's Family Name: ***
Father's Name: ***
Family Name: ***
Mother's Name: ***
Spouse's Name: ***
Marriage Date: ***
Children: ***
Occupation: Guard commander of Ta'neek
Miscellaneous Information:
He has a long scar running over his right eye, but it did not blind him in that eye.
Books: TBG

Gakoal

Race: Uthuk-Nari
Sex: Male
Birth-Death: ***
Height: ***
Hair Color: ***
Eye Color: ***
Family Name: ***
Father's Name: ***
Mother's Family Name: ***
Mother's Name: ***
Spouse's Name: ***
Marriage Date: ***
Children: ***
Occupation: ***

Miscellaneous Information:

He was one of four, with the others being Da'kaalth, Canku, and Za'kah, who traveled with Syry's army to lay siege to Lo'karan. He was 1 of 21 who joined Syry to fight alongside her and free her family's kingdom.

Books: TBG

G'ka'tu

Race: Uthuk-Nari
Sex: Male
Birth-Death: ***
Height: ***
Hair Color: ***
Eye Color: ***
Family Name: ***
Father's Name: ***
Mother's Family Name: ***
Mother's Name: ***
Spouse's Name: ***
Marriage Date: ***
Children: ***
Occupation: ***
Miscellaneous Information:

He was 1 of 21 who joined Syry to fight alongside her and free her family's kingdom.

Books: TBG

Hal

Race: Elf
Sex: Male
Birth-Death: ***

Height: ***
Hair Color: ***
Eye Color: ***
Father's Family Name: ***
Father's Name: ***
Family Name: ***
Mother's Name: ***
Spouse's Name: Tina/Neela
Marriage Date: ***
Children: ***
Occupation: Shopkeeper and tailor
Miscellaneous Information:
He owns the Silken Seam, a tailor shop, with his wife,
Tina.
Books: TBG

Ha'thap Clan Ta'lo'c

Race: Uthuk-Nari
Sex: Male
Birth-Death: ***
Height: 8ft+
Hair Color: ***
Eye Color: ***
Family Name: ***
Father's Name: ***
Mother's Family Name: ***
Mother's Name: ***
Spouse's Name: Arawa
Marriage Date: ***
Children: ***
Occupation: Armorer

Hess

Race: Human
Sex: Male
Birth-Death: ***
Height: ***
Hair Color: ***
Eye Color: ***
Family Name: ***
Father's Name: ***
Mother's Family Name: ***
Mother's Name: ***
Spouse's Name: ***
Marriage Date: ***
Children: ***
Occupation: Warlord
Miscellaneous Information:
A'kull killed him in the village of Ket. He and his band of
men had been killing, raiding, and harassing various
kingdoms.
Books: TBG

Hua-suiiln Clan Nok'noor

Race: Uthuk-Nari
Sex: Male
Birth-Death: (b.)7th of Wróżka Śmierci 4608{UN} (7th of
December 1108)-(d.)?

Height: ***
Hair Color: ***
Eye Color: Bluish-purple
Family Name: Clan Nok'noor
Father's Name: ***
Mother's Family Name: ***
Mother's Name: ***
Spouse's Name: Maisie Clan Falcon
Marriage Date: ***
Children: ***
Occupation: ***
Miscellaneous Information:
He was 1 of 21 who joined Syry to fight alongside her and free her family's kingdom. His eyes can change to red when angry or when his body is healing. A Vampire bit him during the Underlings War, but it did not change him in the strictest sense.
Books: AAC, ADG, TBG

Hycis

Race: Elf
Sex: Female
Birth-Death: ***
Height: ***
Hair Color: ***
Eye Color: ***
Father's Family Name: ***
Father's Name: ***
Family Name: ***
Mother's Name: ***
Spouse's Name: ***

Marriage Date: ***
Children: ***
Occupation: ***
Miscellaneous Information: ***
Books: TBG

Koyla

Race: Human
Sex: Male
Birth-Death: (b.)?-(d.)28th of June 1247
Height: ***
Hair Color: ***
Eye Color: ***
Father's Family Name: ***
Father's Name: Vortigern
Mother's Family Name: ***
Mother's Name: ***
Spouse's Name: ***
Marriage Date: ***
Children: ***
Occupation: Warlord
Miscellaneous Information:
Killed by Syry at the battle of Alloa but was able to strike
at the right moment, a strike that was mortal to Syry.
Books: TBG

Kul'seair

Race: Uthuk-Nari
Sex: Male
Birth-Death: (b.)2502{UN}-(d.)4777{UN} (1277)
Height: ***

Hair Color: ***
Eye Color: ***
Father's Family Name: ***
Father's Name: ***
Mother's Family Name: ***
Mother's Name: ***
Spouse's Name: Aurae Clan Ailsa
Marriage Date: ***
Children: Meesha'ka; Ella
Occupation: ***
Miscellaneous Information:
He was the oldest of the Uthuk-Nari when he died at the age of 2,275. He was 1 of 21 who joined Syry to fight alongside her and free her family's kingdom. He is Syry's grandfather, although he did not tell her for many years.
Books: TBG

Laiex Clan Heir'ic

Race: Elf
Sex: Male
Birth-Death: ***
Height: ***
Hair Color: ***
Eye Color: ***
Father's Family Name: ***
Father's Name: ***
Family Name: Clan Heir'ic
Mother's Name: ***
Spouse's Name: ***
Marriage Date: ***
Children: ***

Occupation: General, rebel leader.
Miscellaneous Information:
He served under King Danu and Queen Ella. Later, he served Syry until her death.
Books: TBG

Lomman

Race: Elf
Sex: Male
Birth-Death: ***
Height: ***
Hair Color: ***
Eye Color: ***
Father's Family Name: ***
Father's Name: ***
Family Name: ***
Mother's Name: ***
Spouse's Name: ***
Marriage Date: ***
Children: ***
Occupation: Elder
Miscellaneous Information: ***
Books: TBG

Lyra Clan Falcon

Race: Elf
Sex: Female
Birth-Death: ***
Height: ***
Hair Color: ***
Eye Color: ***

Father's Family Name: ***
Father's Name: ***
Family Name: Clan Falcon
Mother's Name: ***
Spouse's Name: Syry Clan Ailsa
Marriage Date: ***
Children: Maisie (1248)
Occupation: ***
Miscellaneous Information:
Did give birth to a daughter conceived with Syry not long
after the Alloa battle.
Books: TBG

Maith

Race: Elf
Sex: Female
Birth-Death: ***
Height: ***
Hair Color: ***
Eye Color: ***
Father's Family Name: ***
Father's Name: ***
Family Name: ***
Mother's Name: ***
Spouse's Name: ***
Marriage Date: ***
Children: ***
Occupation: ***
Miscellaneous Information: ***
Books: TBG

Ma'yta

Race: Uthuk-Nari
Sex: Female
Birth-Death: ***
Height: ***
Hair Color: ***
Eye Color: ***
Family Name: ***
Father's Name: ***
Mother's Family Name: ***
Mother's Name: ***
Spouse's Name: A'kull Clan Ta'lo'c
Marriage Date: ***
Children: E'yti
Occupation: ***
Miscellaneous Information:
An older sister to Sewa.
Books: TBG

Meesha'ka Clan Ailsa

Race: Elf/Uthuk-Nari
Sex: Female
Birth-Death: ***
Height: ***
Hair Color: ***
Eye Color: Royal Purple
Father's Family Name: ***
Father's Name: Kul'seair
Family Name: Clan Ailsa
Mother's Name: Aurae
Spouse's Name: ***

Marriage Date: ***
Children: ***
Occupation: Seer
Miscellaneous Information:
An older sister to Ella.
Books: TBG

Mi'jei

Race: Uthuk-Nari
Sex: Female
Birth-Death: ***
Height: ***
Hair Color: ***
Eye Color: ***
Family Name: ***
Father's Name: ***
Mother's Family Name: ***
Mother's Name: ***
Spouse's Name: ***
Marriage Date: ***
Children: ***
Occupation: Armorer
Miscellaneous Information:
She is a master armorer among the Uthuk-Nari.
Books: TBG

Morna

Race: Raven
Sex: Female
Birth-Death: (b.)?-(d.)2nd of Caladh (July) 1247
Height: ***

Hair Color: White
Eye Color: Deep Royal Sapphire Blue
Miscellaneous Information:
She was found as a fledgling by Syry on the Snow Raven Mountain.
Books: TBG

No'jouit

Race: Uthuk-Nari
Sex: Male
Birth-Death: ***
Height: ***
Hair Color: ***
Eye Color: ***
Family Name: ***
Father's Name: ***
Mother's Family Name: ***
Mother's Name: ***
Spouse's Name: ***
Marriage Date: ***
Children: ***
Occupation: Swordsmith
Miscellaneous Information:
He is a master Sword smith among the Uthuk-Nari.
Books: TBG

Ochui

Race: Uthuk-Nari
Sex: Male
Birth-Death: ***
Height: ***

Hair Color: ***
Eye Color: ***
Family Name: ***
Father's Name: ***
Mother's Family Name: ***
Mother's Name: ***
Spouse's Name: ***
Marriage Date: ***
Children: ***
Occupation: ***
Miscellaneous Information:
He is the oldest of the group that met A'kull in Kent. He
was 1 of 21 who joined Syry to fight alongside her and free
her family's kingdom.
Books: TBG

Sewa

Race: Uthuk-Nari
Sex: Female
Birth-Death: ***
Height: ***
Hair Color: ***
Eye Color: ***
Family Name: ***
Father's Name: ***
Mother's Family Name: ***
Mother's Name: ***
Spouse's Name: ***
Marriage Date: ***
Children: ***
Occupation: ***

Miscellaneous Information:
Younger sister to Ma'yta and sister-in-law to A'kull. She was 1 of 21 who joined Syry to fight alongside her and free her family's kingdom.
Books: TBG

Sontar

Race: Elf
Sex: Male
Birth-Death: ***
Height: ***
Hair Color: ***
Eye Color: ***
Father's Family Name: ***
Father's Name: ***
Family Name: ***
Mother's Name: ***
Spouse's Name: ***
Marriage Date: ***
Children: ***
Occupation: ***
Miscellaneous Information: ***
Books: TBG

Syry Clan Ailsa

Race: Elf
Sex: Female
Birth-Death: (b.)Sneachta Sióg (January) 1216-(d.)28th of Sciatháin Féileacán (June) 1247
Height: ***
Hair Color: Fire-kissed blond

Eye Color: Royal Blue
Father's Family Name: Clan Ayr
Father's Name: Danu
Family Name: Clan Ailsa
Mother's Name: Ella
Spouse's Name: Lyra Clan Falcon
Marriage Date: 1246
Children: Maisie(1248)
Occupation: Queen, fallen princess
Miscellaneous Information:
She can vanish from sight. Her sword is made of pure Trinthi'ium; its crosstree is shaped like a raven's head with sapphires for its eyes. The Elvish inscription on her sword reads *Shadows Ghost in Blood and Honor*. Her banner is a white raven upon a purple field. A'kull raised her at the Uthuk-Nari's home in Śnieżna Góra Kruka or Snow Raven Mountain. She sired a daughter with Lyra after the Alloa battle. She often wore black-dyed leather pants and a blue Elven silk shirt with a tooth of a Hakari (Stonefeather Cat) hanging from a silk choker. Her wedding gown was red and black.
Books: TBG

Tah'kainn

Race: Uthuk-Nari
Sex: Male
Birth-Death: (b.)?-(d.)20th of Delikatny 5345 {UN} (20th of March 1845)
Height: ***
Hair Color: ***
Eye Color: ***

Family Name: ***
Father's Name: ***
Mother's Family Name: ***
Mother's Name: ***
Spouse's Name: ***
Marriage Date: ***
Children: ***
Occupation: ***
Miscellaneous Information:
He was 1 of 21 who joined Syry to fight alongside her and free her family's kingdom
Books: TBG

Takari

Race: Elf
Sex: Female
Birth-Death: ***
Height: ***
Hair Color: ***
Eye Color: ***
Father's Family Name: ***
Father's Name: Cohnal
Family Name: ***
Mother's Name: ***
Spouse's Name: ***
Marriage Date: ***
Children: ***
Occupation: ***
Miscellaneous Information:

She was a skilled mounted archer and was the leader of
mounted archers who traveled with Syry as she headed for
Lo'karan after being crowned queen.
Books: TBG

Tee

Race: Elf
Sex: Male
Birth-Death: (b.)1203~-(d.)?
Height: ***
Hair Color: ***
Eye Color: ***
Father's Family Name: ***
Father's Name: ***
Family Name: ***
Mother's Name: ***
Spouse's Name: ***
Marriage Date: ***
Children: ***
Occupation: Blacksmith apprentice
Miscellaneous Information:
He was a young Apprentice to Ha'thap and was 13 at the
time of meeting A'kull and baby Syry.
Books: TBG

Te'jo

Race: Uthuk-Nari
Sex: Male
Birth-Death: ***
Height: ***
Hair Color: ***

Eye Color: ***
Family Name: ***
Father's Name: ***
Mother's Family Name: ***
Mother's Name: ***
Spouse's Name: ***
Marriage Date: ***
Children: ***
Occupation: ***
Miscellaneous Information:
His favored weapon is the battle-ax. He was 1 of 21 who joined Syry to fight alongside her and free her family's kingdom.
Books: TBG

T'hetha

Race: Uthuk-Nari
Sex: Female
Birth-Death: ***
Height: ***
Hair Color: ***
Eye Color: ***
Family Name: ***
Father's Name: ***
Mother's Family Name: ***
Mother's Name: ***
Spouse's Name: ***
Marriage Date: ***
Children: ***
Occupation: ***
Miscellaneous Information:

She was 1 of 21 who joined Syry to fight alongside her and free her family's kingdom.

Books: TBG

Tina/Neela

Race: Elf
Sex: Female
Birth-Death: ***
Height: ***
Hair Color: ***
Eye Color: ***
Father's Family Name: ***
Father's Name: ***
Family Name: ***
Mother's Name: ***
Spouse's Name: Hal
Marriage Date: ***
Children: ***
Occupation: Tailor, shopkeeper, mage
Miscellaneous Information:
Her birth name is Neela. She once served King Danu and Queen Ella at their court in Totia. Owns the Silken Seam, a tailor shop, with her husband, Hal.

Books: TBG

Toran Clan Hanen

Race: Human
Sex: Male
Birth-Death: ***
Height: ***
Hair Color: ***

Eye Color: ***
Family Name: Clan Hanen
Father's Name: ***
Mother's Family Name: ***
Mother's Name: ***
Spouse's Name: ***
Marriage Date: ***
Children: ***
Occupation: Lord of Kent
Miscellaneous Information: ***
Books: TBG

Unka

Race: Uthuk-Nari
Sex: Male
Birth-Death: ***
Height: ***
Hair Color: ***
Eye Color: ***
Family Name: ***
Father's Name: ***
Mother's Family Name: ***
Mother's Name: ***
Spouse's Name: ***
Marriage Date: ***
Children: ***
Occupation: ***
Miscellaneous Information:
He was 1 of 21 who joined Syry to fight alongside her and free her family's kingdom.
Books: TBG

Vah'taar

Race: Uthuk-Nari
Sex: Male
Birth-Death: ***
Height: ***
Hair Color: ***
Eye Color: ***
Family Name: ***
Father's Name: ***
Mother's Family Name: ***
Mother's Name: ***
Spouse's Name: ***
Marriage Date: ***
Children: ***
Occupation: ***
Miscellaneous Information:
He was 1 of 21 who joined Syry to fight alongside her and free her family's kingdom
Books: TBG

Vah'tial

Race: Uthuk-Nari
Sex: Male
Birth-Death: ***
Height: ***
Hair Color: ***
Eye Color: ***
Family Name: ***
Father's Name: ***
Mother's Family Name: ***
Mother's Name: ***

Spouse's Name: ***
Marriage Date: ***
Children: ***
Occupation: ***
Miscellaneous Information: ***
Books: TBG

Ya'jea-Bo

Race: Uthuk-Nari
Sex: Male
Birth-Death: ***
Height: ***
Hair Color: ***
Eye Color: ***
Family Name: ***
Father's Name: ***
Mother's Family Name: ***
Mother's Name: ***
Spouse's Name: ***
Marriage Date: ***
Children: ***
Occupation: ***
Miscellaneous Information:
He was 1 of 21 who joined Syry to fight alongside her and free her family's kingdom.
Books: TBG

Ya'tui

Race: Uthuk-Nari
Sex: Female
Birth-Death: ***

Height: ***
Hair Color: ***
Eye Color: ***
Family Name: ***
Father's Name: ***
Mother's Family Name: ***
Mother's Name: ***
Spouse's Name: ***
Marriage Date: ***
Children: ***
Occupation: ***
Miscellaneous Information:
She was 1 of 21 who joined Syry to fight alongside her and
free her family's kingdom.
Books: TBG

Za'kah

Race: Uthuk-Nari
Sex: Male
Birth-Death: ***
Height: ***
Hair Color: ***
Eye Color: ***
Family Name: ***
Father's Name: ***
Mother's Family Name: ***
Mother's Name: ***
Spouse's Name: ***
Marriage Date: ***
Children: ***
Occupation: ***

Miscellaneous Information:

He was 1 of 21 who joined Syry to fight alongside her and free her family's kingdom. He was one of four, with the others being Da'kaalth, Canku, and Gakoal, who traveled with Syry's army to lay siege to Lo'karan.

Books: TBG

About the Author

Tristan R. Waters

Tristan R. Waters has lived in New Mexico his whole life, having been born and raised in the Sandia Mountains east of Albuquerque, New Mexico. He has spent much of his free time writing fantasy, with many never coming to fruition, with the exception now being *Birth of a Goddess*. When he's not writing his medieval fantasies, he's working on graduate work, tinkering on some sort of hobby project, or getting out and off-roading in his Jeep Wrangler. He is a lover of history, focusing on the Middle Ages and the Second World War, with many shelves filled with books on these subjects.